GOD'S STEPFATHER

by
Andrew R Guyatt

SOURCES

This story traces the birth and childhood of Jesus Christ from the viewpoint of his stepfather Joseph (referred to here informally as Joe). It is based on the biblical accounts, principally Matthew 1:18 to 2:23 and Luke 1:5 to 2:53. For background material, I referred to the Jewish historian Flavius Josephus who was born in 37 AD. The information was taken from "The Antiquities of the Jews," Book 17:6 to 10, and "The Wars of the Jews," Book 1:33 to Book 2:5.

ACKNOWLEDGMENTS

I am very grateful to the Midhurst Writers' Group who listened patiently week after week to a reading of this novel and made many helpful suggestions. Also, I had assistance and encouragement from my late cousin Mary Batchelor and several friends including Jean Clark.

Finally and by no means least, I must thank my wife, Sue, who gave expert advice as a retired nurse and midwife. Her forbearance was exceptional as was that of my children: Helen, Tom, Matilda, Alice, and Barney.

Cover designed by
GRAFICA BY THE SEA
Littlehampton UK
BN17 6JU

FOREWORD

Joseph, husband of Mary and stepfather of Jesus, is famously silent in all his appearances in Scripture. Not one word do we hear him say, as he rises to the challenges of a mysteriously pregnant fiancée; his wife giving birth in a makeshift stable; homelessness, exile and life as a refugee; and bringing up as his own a stepson with a unique Messianic vocation. Perhaps we hear the accounts so often, in readings at carol services and during the Christmas season, that we take for granted the part played by this exceptional and courageous man. In this novel, Joseph is silent no more. Immersed in Scriptural knowledge and lightly-worn historical research, underpinned by a deep personal faith, Dr Guyatt gives a voice to the voiceless. He brings to vivid life this man who had so important a role to fulfil.

As he follows Joseph's story, Dr Guyatt does not shy away from the difficult, even painful, aspects that it contains. This is no oversimplified Sunday-school tale, but a nuanced and psychologically shrewd depiction. We are shown a man who grows in faith and stature, responsive to God's call, while remaining fully human and subject to the qualms and doubts and human jealousies which beset us all from time to time. That is one of the most encouraging aspects of this lively and moving book: we are shown how Jesus was born into a real family with all its imperfections and that his early life was not the stuff of fairy tales.

To write on such a subject, where the writings of the Jewish historian Josephus supplement the Scriptural accounts, calls for a keen historical sense. Dr Guyatt's knowledge and research inform the novel unobtrusively; the learning is handled with a delightful lightness of touch. Similarly, his strong and lived-out personal faith is held with a quiet confidence which does not need to hector. This is a work which the Christian reader can relish, and also a work to captivate and intrigue readers whatever their perspective.

As a lay-person of Christian faith, who am biblically literate but not a theologian, I found this book a page-turner. I became completely involved with Joseph and his predicaments. Dr Guyatt paints for us a richly detailed canvas, with Mary and Jesus, as well as a host of minor characters, each coming to life and illuminating the big picture. I absorbed, almost without realizing it, some background history of which I was unaware. That will now bring added richness to the birth narratives and stories of Jesus's early life when I read them or hear them in public worship. Joseph has spoken, and it is a treat to hear his voice, imaginatively reconstructed by Dr Guyatt. I was reminded of the maxim of Ignatius Loyola: 'God in all things'. That is what we were shown in this compelling novel.

Caroline Myddelton

MA (Oxon); Barrister-at-law; Extra-Mural Certificate in Religious Studies, University of London (Distinction); Advanced Diploma in Professional Training and Development, Homerton College Cambridge (Distinction); Head of Training (retired), Inner London Magistrates' Courts Service.

TABLE OF CONTENTS

CHAPTER ONE

I suppose, really, I could have stopped her going. After all, we were betrothed, and in our culture that's as good as being married—well, apart from sleeping together. She was my responsibility now, and she had to do what I told her.

She'd come round to the workshop with some bread and cheese for my lunch, then she said, "I'm sorry, Joe, but I've got to go away. We'll have to put the wedding off for a bit!"

The words didn't seem to make sense, so she tried again. "I'm sorry, Joe! But we've got to put the wedding off."

I felt like I'd been hit in the stomach. "But Mary ... it's next week!"

"Look, I'm sorry, Joe, but something's happened. I'll tell you about it as soon as I can. Just for now, though, I've got to go down to Judea."

"To Judea? All that way? You must be joking."

"No, I'm not. You see, I've got a cousin down there, name of Elizabeth; she's married to one of the priests and she's having a baby. She needs me."

"That's the first I've heard of her!"

"Well, I've only met her a couple of times myself. But it's her first baby, and she's getting on a bit."

"Are you out of your mind? There must be a whole load of women down there falling over themselves to help. Why on earth do you have to go?"

"Look, Joe, I can't explain now—you've just got to trust me. I promise I'll be back soon, and then I'll tell you all about it."

I stood there with my mouth open. This was my girl! I'd fancied her ever since we were kids, and we'd been betrothed for a year. I reckoned I knew her pretty well by now; she was always the same, quiet and looking to help everyone, never trying to get her own way. But now this—she must have changed overnight!

Then I started shouting. "Look, Mary, don't you want to marry me? Are you going to break our contract?"

"Oh no, I want you, Joe, more than anything! It's ... well, something's happened, and I need to sort it out."

"Something's happened? What, for goodness sake?"

She stood twisting her hands together, and I saw she was close to tears. "Well, Joe ... it's a bit difficult. It's not that I don't trust you or anything, but this is a woman's thing and I'd like to talk it through with Elizabeth."

"But ... well ... have you told your parents? What have they got to say?"

"I had a word with Mother. She wasn't too keen on me going and tried to talk me out of it. But she said since you're my fiancé, it's up to you to make the final decision."

"So how long are you intending to be gone?"

"I'm afraid I don't know. It may be a month or more."

"What, a whole month? What do you expect me to do all that time? And how on earth do you intend to get down there? You can't wander off on your own; it's just not safe."

"A couple of priests from Gath Heber are due down in Jerusalem to do their service at the Temple. I went up to see them this morning and arranged to join their party."

I blinked. This was extraordinary. Mary was the very last person I could imagine making such an arrangement; she was so shy. She must be really serious about this trip to go to that trouble.

"Well, Joe, may I go?"

She was looking at me in that special way she had, head on one side with a half-smile, and there was nothing I could do.

"Well, I suppose if you have to. But get back as soon as you can. I'm going to miss you."

"Me too."

I stood there a long time after she walked out. Then I slammed down the hammer I'd been using. "She's mad! Stark raving mad! Dashing down there to help a stranger—and what about me, for goodness sake? Don't I need her just as much? What am I going to tell everybody?"

I had a word with Mother, but she hadn't heard anything.

"Are you sure you got that right, Joe? She was round here yesterday morning and she didn't say anything. In fact, she was full of the wedding and we had a good chat."

"She must have changed her mind!"

"I don't think so. Obviously, something very important must have come up. If I get a chance, I'll have a word with her."

I hardly slept that night; I couldn't imagine what had gotten into her. But the more I thought about it, the more certain I was that she'd break her betrothal vows. I really loved that girl, and if I lost her, there'd be nothing left to live for.

The next morning, I saw her coming up the road toward us, but I was so scared about what she might say that I kept out of the way till she'd gone. Then eventually, I plucked up the courage to speak to Mother.

"Did you manage to talk her out of this trip of hers?"

"No, I'm sorry, Joe; I didn't."

I groaned. "If only I'd been firmer with her!"

"I doubt it would have made any difference. She's dead set on it; in fact, she thinks that God's told her to go!"

"She never said that to me."

"I doubt you gave her the chance. She said you were very annoyed."

"Well, I was looking forward to getting married."

"So is Mary. You know she loves you just as much as ever, despite your behavior—it's just that you'll have to wait a bit."

"While she makes a fool of me in front of everyone!"

"Oh Joe, please! You know she's not like that!"

"Well, I hope not. And anyway, what's all this about God speaking to her?"

"I don't know. She didn't tell me, but it obviously meant a lot. My guess is she needs time to think things over, so that's why she's going away."

"But I can't believe it! God speaking to her! She's only a girl!"

To my surprise, Mother laughed. "Now look, Joe, women matter to God too! Don't forget how Miriam led the worship after our fathers crossed the Red Sea!"

"But she's so young."

"God likes talking to young people. Samuel was just a lad when he called him."

"Well, maybe, but I don't like her travelling all that way. You know what those Roman soldiers are like; see a pretty girl and they'll grab her. Either that or it'll be the bandits!"

Mother sighed. "Now listen to me, Joe! If God's sending her, he's going to look after her and bring her back safely! I wish you'd been here earlier, then you could have had a word with her yourself. She hung around as long as she could in case you turned up, but she couldn't keep those folks waiting."

"I'll go and catch her up."

"You'll have to hurry then; she went quite a time ago."

I ran as fast as I could, but when I got to the road at the bottom of the hill, there was no sign of her. I had a long hot climb back up to the village and I began regretting my behavior, but there was no way I could put that right now.

I ran into my oldest brother, Simon, when I got back. Since Father died, he'd kept an eye on me and got me out of

5

a few scrapes.

"Joe, what's this I hear about Mary? Mother was saying she's gone off to see her cousin down south."

"That's right. I don't know, but for some reason she wanted to go."

"That seems a bit odd with the wedding coming up. Did she say why she was going?"

"Well, eh … No. She just said it was very important and that her cousin's having a baby."

"She should be stopping at home to get everything ready."

"Well, yes, I know, but she did ask if she could go."

"I'm very surprised you agreed. Remember, you're going to be head of the household, and you need to start as you mean to carry on. She's expected to do what you tell her and not follow her own ideas. No one's going to think much of you if you can't control your own wife."

That set me worrying again. Until two days ago, everything was going well; Mary seemed so gentle and obedient, just the sort of girl any man looks for. But perhaps, after all, she had a rebellious streak, and once we were married, I would be in for a surprise. But then I got some good news.

Two weeks later I happened to meet one of the men who had gone with the priests from Gath Heber down to Jerusalem.

"Ah yes, you must be the lucky man who's going to marry that Mary who came with us. You know you've got someone special there, and she obviously loves you—she kept talking about you. I hope you two will be very happy."

"Thanks, I'm glad to hear that. But tell me, did she manage to meet up with her cousin?"

"Yes, it worked out just right for her. Her cousin's husband's a priest too, and he'd just finished his week at the Temple, so she went back with him. Funny old man he was, didn't say anything, but I'm sure she'll be safe with him."

I was counting on Mary returning home in a month, but it was three before she turned up, and long before that, I was convinced I'd never see her again. And my mood wasn't helped by my friends' comments.

"What have you done with that girl of yours, Joe?"

"You know you shouldn't let a woman out of your sight."

"Do you think she's coming back?"

"Maybe she's taken up with a Roman soldier!"

But if I found the waiting and the remarks bad enough, things were just about to get a whole heap worse.

I was in the workshop finishing off an urgent job before the light went. Then suddenly I noticed her standing in the doorway smiling at me.

"I've come back, Joe!"

I should have told her how thrilled I was to see her; instead I muttered, "You took your time about it, didn't you?"

She winced. "I'm very, very sorry, Joe. I wanted to come back earlier, but Elizabeth needed me."

"Meaning, I suppose, that I didn't?"

As soon as I had spoken, I regretted it. I saw she was close to tears. "I'm sorry, love," I blurted out, "that was a stupid thing to say … It's been a bad day. But it's great to see you."

"It's lovely to be back. I've been longing for you."

I went to give her a hug, but she stepped back. Suddenly my knees felt weak and I felt scared. "Mary, what's wrong?"

"Nothing, Joe, it's just that …"

"Don't you love me anymore?"

"Of course I do. More than ever. It's only that … well … I've got something I ought to tell you." She pulled my sleeve. "Let's go up the hill. It'll be easier to talk up there."

I can still see that evening like it was yesterday. It was spring with flowers everywhere and the setting sun making everything look pink, and I could see the shadows showing up the ridges on the hillside, but I had an awful feeling that everything was about to end.

Then Mary turned to me; I could see she was trembling.

"Joe, love. I saw an angel!"

I didn't know what to say so I stared at her.

She lowered her head. "Joe, please listen to me. Look, I've seen an angel and he told me … He's told me that … well … I'm going to have a baby!"

CHAPTER TWO

It wasn't my child!

That at least I knew. However much I'd been tempted to sleep with her, I'd resolved to wait till we got married—and this was my reward!

I'd trusted her! I'd shared everything with her, even the secrets I hadn't told anyone else, and now she'd betrayed me.

"You've tricked me," I shouted. "You tricked me and I trusted you!"

She clutched my arm. "Joe, it's not like that ..."

I shook her off. "Not like that? What do you mean? You think I'm stupid or something?"

"Joe, please listen to me. I've got to tell you what happened."

"I know what happened all right. You had it off with a bloke who got you in the family way, and now you have the nerve to come back to me!"

"But Joe, please let me tell you. It's God himself who's the father of my child, not a man!"

I'd heard some stories in my time, but this topped them all. "What?" I shouted.

"God made me pregnant himself! An angel told me, and his Holy Spirit came over me although I'm still a virgin."

She must have been stark raving mad! But when I looked at her, all I saw were her eyes brimming with tears and pleading. Any other time, I'd have wanted to put my arm round her; instead, I blundered away up the hill.

Who was the father? Did he live in the village? I started working through the local men in my mind, wondering who it could be.

Had she been raped? I'd kill whoever did it with my bare hands! But if so, why hadn't she told me?

Maybe it hadn't happened here at all. Was that why she left in a hurry? That story of visiting her cousin was just a pack of lies: she'd gone to be with her lover, but when he found she was pregnant, he threw her out and she'd had the cheek to come back and expect me to cover for her.

I stayed out till dark, by turns raging and feeling humiliated. But despite everything, I still couldn't forget the way she'd looked at me.

Mother was waiting when I got in. "You're late. Your supper's on the table."

"Thank you, Mother; I'll eat it later."

I turned my face away from her, but it was no good, she knew something was wrong.

"How's Mary? I heard she's back."

"That's right," I grunted.

"Have you had a chance to speak to her?"

"Yes."

"Is something wrong?"

I burst into tears then, sobbing like a baby. She pulled me to her and began stroking my hair like she did when I was a boy. I was dreading her questions, but instead she let me go.

"Don't forget," she said. "God loves you—and so does Mary!"

I stumbled up the ladder to the hay loft that I used to share with my brothers. But I didn't expect to get much sleep that night.

I still couldn't believe it—Mary of all people! Rumor had it that some girls in the village enjoyed the odd romp, but surely not her! Why, she would even slip away if someone started telling a dirty story, and she kept her eyes down when there were strange men around.

When I'd first gotten interested in her, I thought her too shy to respond, but bit by bit, I won her confidence and realized she was the one for me. The day we were betrothed was the proudest of my life—I'd got myself the most wonderful girl in Galilee!

But what should I do now?

I could wash my hands of her and denounce her publicly. I'd be quite within my rights, but there was the danger I'd be held up to ridicule and labelled a cuckold.

Even worse, what would happen to her?

I still loved her dearly despite what she had done, and I couldn't bear to hurt her. If I shamed her openly, she might be stoned or at the least driven out of the village. More than likely she'd finish up as a prostitute in Sepphoris, the town

11

just over the hill.

No, whatever it cost, somehow I must get her out of the way quietly.

There was her cousin Elizabeth. It was just possible she would take her back; it would be far enough away to avoid gossip. But her husband was a priest; how would he feel about having an immoral girl around the place?

Another option was Capernaum down by the lake; I'd worked there briefly two years back for some Greek folk. They were more relaxed about moral lapses than us Jews, and if I made it worth their while, they might take her in. I'd been saving up for the new home, but I wouldn't need that silver now.

I laid down on the straw, though after what I'd been through, I didn't expect to get any sleep. But eventually I dropped off ...

You can't describe an angel. If you say you've seen one, folk think you're mad and laugh—but this was the biggest shock of my life! There was this huge man standing in front of me, blazing bright with all the colors of the rainbow.

Scared isn't the word for it—I thought I'd been struck by lightning. I hid my head under my cloak, but the light was so bright I could still see him!

All I knew about angels came from the old stories we heard in synagogue, but I didn't need any persuading I was seeing one now! I had an overwhelming sense of holiness that made me feel filthy; more than likely I'd be burnt up on the spot.

Then he spoke. It sounded like a thunderclap and yet somehow gentle.

He began by addressing me by name, "Joseph son of David." That may not sound like much, but it meant a lot to me. I may be just a humble carpenter, but I'm very proud of my ancestry—why, I can trace it right back to that special king!

I plucked up my courage and took another peep at him. He was smiling as he spoke. "Don't be afraid to take Mary as your wife because the baby she's carrying was given to her by the Holy Spirit. She's going to have a boy, and I want you to call him Jesus because he's going to save his people from their sins."

And that was it! As I stared at him, he vanished just like that.

For a moment, I thought I was dreaming; then I realized I was wide awake. My first thought was that he had woken half the village, but all I could hear was the breeze stirring the leaves of the olive tree outside.

To say I felt stunned is putting it mildly. I lay back for a long time trying to get my head round what had happened. But the funny thing was that although the angel had disappeared, I still felt him beside me explaining things.

One thing was sure; however incredible it seemed, Mary had told me the truth. She had seen an angel, and God's spirit had made her pregnant. Hers would be no ordinary baby but someone special.

A phrase came back to me from one of the prophets I studied in Hebrew class. "A virgin will become pregnant and have a son, and they will call him Immanuel, which means 'God with us.'" Ezra, our rabbi, explained this referred to the Messiah, the great hero who was going to be born one day and who would rescue our nation.

Maybe he was coming now!

I couldn't believe it—was my Mary really going to be his mother? How could this happen to an ordinary girl like her?

But as I pondered, things began to make sense. She had hurried off to see Elizabeth so she could talk about the baby and maybe have a word with her husband. As he was a priest, he would know the truth if anyone did.

But she must have dreaded telling me. And my face burned as I remembered how I'd treated her and the things I'd said. The sooner I apologized the better—that is, if she'd listen to me. If we were going to get married like the angel said, we'd have to sort things out between us somehow.

Then I thought about the name I was to give the baby. A boy in the village was called Jesus, and Ezra had explained it came from the Hebrew Joshua, which means, "God saves."

The original Joshua had been a great man. After Moses died, he took the Israelites across the Jordan to capture the land. He had saved his people, and somehow that fitted in with what the angel had said about our Jesus saving his people from their sins. I couldn't say I understood that last bit, but I hoped Mary could explain it to me.

I must have fallen asleep then, and the sun was high in the sky when I stirred. I felt really happy and started singing as I pulled on my robe.

I was still humming away as I came down the ladder. Then I caught sight of Mother looking startled and it started me giggling. I laughed till I cried.

Then I went round to Mary's home. I was chatting to her parents when she walked in, and she flinched when she saw me.

"Joseph wants to fix a new day for the wedding," her mother explained. "And the sooner we get it over with, the better, before you go and change your mind again!"

Mary's jaw dropped, and she stood staring at me till her mother got irritated. "What's got into you, my girl? You ought to be delighted he's still interested in you after the way you've messed him around!"

She took a moment to reply. "I'll be ready whenever he wants."

As I started back down the hill, she came after me. But I felt so ashamed that I kept walking and she had to run to catch up.

"Joe! What's happened? I didn't think you'd want to see me again!"

I couldn't look her in the eye. "Well, Mary, we're betrothed and we're getting married. That's all there is to it."

She stared at the ground. "But didn't you hear what I said yesterday about being pregnant?"

"Yes. But I still think we should go ahead."

'But ... How are you going to feel when I ... I ... when I have the baby?"

I swallowed hard. "Mary, we're going to get married. God wants us to."

She looked so surprised that I laughed. There was nothing for it; I'd have to tell her everything. "You're not going to believe this, but ... well, last night ... I know it sounds crazy ... I saw an angel!"

"You didn't?"

"I did just as sure as I'm here now, and I was scared stiff. He was blazing bright with a huge voice, but somehow he calmed me down and told me that ... well, we should get married and it was all right about the baby."

She grabbed my arm. "Joe! What did he say about him?"

"That the Holy Spirit of God had given him to you and that I was to call him Jesus."

She burst into tears; then I started crying. I told her that I loved her and how ashamed I was of what I'd said. Then she smiled up at me. I'll never know what it is about her, but every time she looks at me like that I'm finished!

"Joe, love! That's what happened to me! I saw an angel too and he told me about the baby. He even gave me the same name!"

I looked round to see if anyone was watching; the street wasn't the best place to talk. So we wandered back up the hill and sat down on some spring grass. Then she began.

CHAPTER THREE

"Joe, darling, I do love you and I was trying my best to get ready for the wedding. But then Gabriel came and nothing's been the same since!"

"Gabriel?" I snapped. "Who's he? I don't know anyone round here called that."

She smiled. "Why, he's an angel who came and visited me. Perhaps he was the same one you saw."

I winced; that experience was all too real. But Mary was still talking.

"It was a real shock seeing him standing there in our kitchen as real as you are. He knew I was scared, so he started by telling me not to be afraid, and he had such a soft voice that I soon calmed down. Then he said how special I was to God."

"All right, but what did he say about the baby?"

"He said the child I would carry would be the Son of the Most High and inherit King David's throne and reign forever."

I looked at her carefully to see if she was joking; however, there was a look of awe in her eyes. "But I mean ... well, doesn't that make him some sort of king?"

"Yes, it does. But it's more than that; he'll be a very special king if he's going to reign forever."

This was too deep for me, but there was an important question I needed answered. "Let's get one thing straight: who's the father? My angel said something about the Holy Spirit of God making you pregnant."

"Yes, that's exactly what Gabriel told me."

"But ... I mean ... well .... Look, you haven't cheated on me, have you?"

"No, Joe, I haven't—you must believe me. I told Gabriel straight out I hadn't slept with a man, but he said the Spirit would come over me so that I could have the baby. He also said he'd be the Son of God."

I shook my head. "That's quite a lot to take in."

"Yes, Joe, but I do know I'm pregnant and also that I'm still a virgin!"

I waited a bit before I spoke again. "Did he say anything else?"

"Yes, he told me about Elizabeth having a baby. Although she seemed too old, she was already six months gone, and if God could do that for her, he could do anything."

"Like you having a baby without sex?"

"Yes, that's just it! All I had to do was agree to be the mother."

"Well, how long did you take to make your mind up?"

"No time at all. I knew straight off it was right, so I bowed and offered myself to God there and then. By the time

I looked up again, Gabriel had gone."

"So this baby of yours, do you think he's going to be Messiah?"

"I'm sure of it."

"But in that case, I mean ... who's going to bring him up?"

"We are!"

I gulped. "But ... the Messiah ... I couldn't possibly be his father! I'm just a humble carpenter!"

She giggled "I'm sorry, Joe; you look so funny! But you don't have to be scared; with God to help you, it's going to be all right. You're a very lucky man; God's given you something really special to do."

"But I'm not good enough!"

"Neither of us are! When I think of all those wonderful women over the years who could have been his mother, and it's going to be me, just an ordinary peasant girl! And I'm not perfect as you'll find out once we're married!"

"But me, Messiah's stepfather!"

She laughed again. "Perhaps I should sing you the psalm I wrote!"

I thought I'd heard everything already that morning, but this left me gawping. "You wrote a psalm?"

"Yes, I know it sounds funny, but it came to me while I was on the way to see Elizabeth. I knew she'd be thrilled to have a baby at her age, and it put me in mind of the story of Hannah."

"You mean Samuel's mother?"

"That's right. For years and years, she'd longed for a child and couldn't have one, then when at last God gave her a son, she sang a wonderful song of praise. It's one of my favorites, and I was singing it as we walked along. Only then the words started changing ..."

"What do you mean 'started changing'?"

"I don't know, but suddenly I found myself singing something new. I was so happy about my baby that it all poured out!"

"What did the others think?"

"Oh, it was really funny. The girl I was with thought I'd gone loopy. She said I had a huge grin on my face and suggested I cover my head to keep the sun off!"

"But can you still remember it?"

"Oh yes! It's stuck in my mind. It goes like this:

"My soul glorifies the Lord
and my spirit rejoices in God my Savior,
for he has been mindful
of the humble state of his servant.
From now every generation will call me blessed,
for the Mighty One has done great things for me—
holy is his name.
His mercy extends to those who fear him,
from generation to generation.
He has performed mighty deeds with his arm,
he has scattered those who are proud in their inmost thoughts,
He has brought down rulers from their thrones

but has lifted up the humble.
He has filled the hungry with good things
but has sent the rich away empty.
He has helped his servant Israel,
remembering to be merciful
to Abraham and his descendants for ever,
even as he said to our fathers."

Mary's often sung it to me since, but I'll never forget that first time. Her voice was as pure as a child, and she seemed to be singing directly to God, like he was a friend. And once she was done, I stayed quiet for a bit as I realized I'd heard a prophecy, as real as any written in our Scriptures.

"That was great," I said at last. "But getting back to Elizabeth, you didn't go all that way just to see if Gabriel was telling the truth?"

"No. I'm sure God sent me." Then she blushed. "I'm sorry, Joe. I should have spoken to you first, but I didn't think you'd understand—it's a lot to ask of a man! And as for my family, I doubt they'd have believed a word."

"But why Elizabeth? You hardly know her."

"Well, if God was doing amazing things for her, she should understand about me. Anyway, it's much easier to talk to a stranger."

"But I can't see how you persuaded your parents into letting you go."

"Well, they certainly weren't happy, but they said it was up to you to make the decision."

"I think you were very brave."

"I didn't feel brave I can tell you! I kept wondering what Elizabeth and her husband—he's Zechariah—would think when I turned up at their door. They might have thrown me out as soon as they heard about the baby."

"So what did happen?"

"It was weird. I knocked and … I know it sounds odd, but I had this awful feeling I'd just been imagining about Gabriel and what he had said. Then a white-haired lady appeared. She was obviously pregnant and though I hadn't seen her for years, I recognized her immediately. So I said 'Hello Elizabeth, remember me? I'm your cousin Mary.'"

"What did she do?"

"That was the amazing thing! She clutched herself and looked at me as if she'd seen a ghost. Then she shouted out, 'Blessed are you among women and blessed is the baby you are carrying …'"

"But how on earth did she know?" I interrupted.

"God must have told her. I hadn't had a chance to say anything. I hadn't even let her know I was coming, and I didn't look pregnant. Why, I'd only found out myself a few days before."

"That must have been quite a relief for you."

"Oh it was, but that wasn't all. She said she felt it was a real honor to receive me and that I was the mother of her Lord! She even told me that when I'd greeted her, her baby had leaped in her womb for joy."

"So you really got a welcome!"

"I did indeed; it was amazing to think that the wife of a priest felt honored to receive me, just a young girl, and that even her unborn baby knew about it. Then she blessed me for believing what the Lord had said to me and told me that it would happen as He said. It was as if she could read my mind and knew about my doubts."

"So what happened then?"

"We hugged each other, then we had a good cry and I sang her my psalm. It was lovely; I could feel God right inside me helping me to pour it out!"

"I hope she liked it?"

"Oh she loved it, and she hugged me again and we cried some more. Then she said she wasn't looking after me properly and that I must stay with them."

"You must have been relieved!"

"I was, but I felt nervous too. You see, their place was small and neat, not like home with all my brothers and sisters messing it up! And what with Zechariah being a priest, we had to be careful about purity."

"That's quite a palaver, isn't it?"

"It is. He's got to keep clean all the time so that he can go up to the Temple when he's needed. He bathed every evening and was very careful about his food."

Then she looked embarrassed. "Well, you know about how women become impure each month. Not that it mattered with the two of us being pregnant, but Elizabeth reckoned she'd have to watch out after the baby was born."

"Did you live with them all the time you were away?"

"Oh yes. I was worried I was in the way, but I think Elizabeth needed me. I helped with the chores, and she had someone to talk to since she couldn't speak to Zechariah."

"Why ever not?"

"Oh didn't I say? He's dumb."

"How dreadful!"

"Yes. He could still write on a tablet, but since she doesn't know her letters, someone had to read it out to her and then write down her reply. So most of the time, he sat in a corner praying."

"Has he been like that long?"

"No, it started just before their baby was conceived. Every six months he goes up to the Temple for a week to be on duty. The priests draw lots to see who's going to offer incense in the Holy Place and he got lucky. But while he was in there, he saw an angel."

"Gabriel again, I suppose?"

"Yes, and he told him that Elizabeth would have a baby despite being so old. The trouble was he didn't believe it, so as a punishment, Gabriel told him he'd be dumb until the baby was born. He stayed in the Holy Place so long the folk outside thought he'd died, and when he did come out, he couldn't say anything. It was only when they fetched him a writing tablet, they discovered what had happened."

"So how did Elizabeth take it?"

"She was thrilled, though it was a pity Zechariah couldn't tell her himself. But being that much older, she found pregnancy quite a strain. In fact, she didn't go outside her front door for five months!"

"And how are you feeling yourself?" I asked, ashamed I hadn't asked her before.

"I'm fine, Joe! I mean, I have been feeling a bit tired and sick, but I'm young and being with Elizabeth worked out well. It's during those first three months that a woman's most likely to lose her baby, and I got a lot more rest there than I would at home."

"But I expect you're glad to be back?"

"Yes, though I must admit I was scared about how I was going to tell you I was pregnant. Elizabeth prayed I'd have the courage and the right words to say and that you'd understand."

I decided to change the subject. "And has Elizabeth had her child?"

"I suppose she must have done by now. I'd have stayed on to help, but I thought it was time to get back, and I heard there was a party heading up to Galilee, so I joined them. Anyway, I reckoned I'd been away long enough; I was really missing you."

For once, there was nothing I could say.

CHAPTER FOUR

If we'd married before Mary went to see Elizabeth, we might have gotten away with it.

It would have still looked a bit quick, but at least we'd have had nine months before the baby was born. But soon, everyone would know he was conceived out of wedlock.

I went to see her parents the next morning, and as I reached the door, I heard her trying to persuade her mother to have the wedding as soon as possible.

"But Mother, it's not fair to keep him waiting."

"Since you've wasted all that time already, what's another few weeks?"

"He won't want to leave it that long."

"Bah! He's waited a year already, a month or so more won't hurt!"

"But Mother ..."

"You should have taken my advice while you had the chance; there were plenty of other young men around. He's got quite a temper, you know; you'll need to watch your step. You should have seen how angry he was when you went away."

"Well, it was pretty hard on him ..."

"It was pretty hard on me too! I was working all hours getting you ready when suddenly you disappeared on a fool errand. Now you expect me to start again!"

"I'm very sorry, Mother ..."

The argument showed no sign of ending, so I decided to leave them to it and slipped away. But back home I found my mother was upset too.

"I'm rather worried about you and Mary. I'm not trying to pry, but I wonder if you're really ready to get married yet."

"I'm sure we are."

"Well, I keep remembering how angry you were when she went away, and it wasn't any better when she got back. What if she goes away again?"

"I'm sure she won't. Anyway, we've sorted that out."

"I do hope so. I couldn't bear it if things went wrong between you."

"They won't," I said hastily.

Mother peered up at me. "Joseph, listen to me. Mary's a really nice girl and I don't want to say anything against her, but maybe she's still a bit young to take on the responsibility of married life. I think it'd be better to wait."

"But we want the wedding now."

"Is that wise? I think it would be better to give her a chance to settle down first. And I'm sure your dear father would have said the same if he were still here."

I went back to the workshop, although I wasn't in the mood for work. I felt I owed it to Mother and Mary's parents to tell them the whole story before the news of her pregnancy broke, but I couldn't think of a way to do it.

I was also in a panic about the wedding arrangements; I was desperate to get them over with before everyone found out about Mary. The village would expect at least a couple of nights' hospitality, and this meant a lot of extra work.

"Look Mother," I said when I got back that evening. "Why don't we just have a drink with the family to celebrate the wedding?"

She was horrified. "What rubbish! You men are all the same! You've no idea what a wedding means to a girl! It's her big day! We'll do better than that!"

"But she did upset the arrangements ..."

"Joseph, I'll hear no more. I'm going to see that she has the best wedding ever!"

And she was as good as her word. It all went very well, the last happy day we had in Nazareth.

Following the usual custom, I waited till dark before going off to collect the bride from her parents' home. My cousin Reuben accompanied me as the "chief companion" and his younger brothers came as the "sons of the bride chamber." We lit our torches and stepped out into the darkness. Then as we approached her door, the lads raised a shout, "The bridegroom's coming."

My arrival was supposed to be a great surprise, but everybody expected me, although they did not know when I would turn up. Suddenly there was a blaze of torches as the neighbors streamed out of their houses to cheer me on, and I imagined Mary quickly slipping into her wedding finery.

While I was waiting her father appeared at the door. "All right, Joe," he said gruffly. "There you are. She's yours now."

Eventually, she emerged looking lovelier than ever, together with her female attendants, and we started to walk together down the hill to Mother's home while my companions and the guests shouted and sang round us.

Our home was already packed with guests eagerly awaiting the ceremony. It was a brief affair at which I confirmed the promises I had made at our betrothal, but something very odd happened. As I gave her a ring, our eyes met, and everyone seemed to disappear, leaving the two of us alone.

Then the singing and dancing began and I even saw Mother tapping her foot. I was enjoying it so much I did not notice how fast time was going, and before I realized it, we were being escorted out to our new home. We were followed by a rowdy cheer from the guests and some pretty frank suggestions.

But this was going to be a very different wedding night.

Mary smiled at me when we were alone together. "I'm sorry, Joe. But we'll just have to wait till he's born."

I nodded. We'd discussed this before.

"But it won't be for long," she whispered.

I knew she had to stay a virgin for the time being, but it would be very hard to treat her like a sister. As she slipped off her robe, I could see the curve of her breasts, and it was as much as I could do not to take her there and then.

A village has a lot of skilled eyes looking for a thickened waist and other telltale signs of pregnancy. Perhaps it was my imagination, but even during our wedding, I thought I saw some women giving Mary searching looks.

Soon, of course, everyone knew and the old women were gleefully counting on their fingers.

I was walking up the street one morning when I saw several men laughing. You know when they've been telling dirty jokes by the way they huddle together, but it was a shock when I realized they were sniggering at me.

"Here's the old goat!"

"Friskier than we took him for!"

"Couldn't wait, eh?"

Then James, who lived three doors up from us, sidled over to me with a smirk on his face. "Heard your Mary's having a baby?"

"Yes," I said stiffly, looking straight ahead.

"Didn't waste much time, did you? Heard she's six months gone already."

"Look, just let me get on, won't you? I've got a job to do."

"Reckon you've done one already!"

I left him still chuckling.

I could feel my fists tightening. How dare he talk to me like that! But what could I do? Tell him about the angel? I'd be a laughingstock. I could imagine the men making the sign of the horns of a cuckold as I went by.

I saw my older sister, Miriam, later. "Joe, there's some stories going round about you and Mary."

"Oh." I grunted.

"They say you didn't wait for the wedding and she's five months pregnant already."

"Well, something like that."

She looked really disappointed. "Oh Joe—how could you? I've been telling everybody it's rubbish. You've let the whole family down! Mother's really upset."

"She knows then?"

"Oh yes, her friends told her. Only she said it wasn't true because you'd never do a thing like that. Now she'll be too ashamed to speak to them again."

Mary was very quiet that evening. I noticed she was turning her head away from me.

"Are you all right?" I said. Then I caught sight of her eye. It was black and almost closed.

"Who's done that to you?" I shouted. "I'll break his neck!"

She held her head for a moment then began to cry. "Joe!" she said between sobs, "it was my mother. She's simply furious about the baby."

"I'll go round and sort her out!"

"No!" She grabbed my arm. "You mustn't go near her. She said she never wanted to see either of us again. I dread to think what she'd do if you turned up!"

"I'll never forgive her for hurting you!"

She pulled me round till we were looking at each other. "Joe. It's my mother you're talking about. She doesn't know what happened, and she wouldn't believe it if she did. You've just got to be patient. Give her time and she'll come round."

"You've got more faith in her than I have! And it's not just her either; my mother's very upset. I just don't know what to do!"

Then Mary smiled, rather carefully because of her painful face. "Joe, why don't we tell her the truth? I think she'll understand. She's the only person in the village who would."

Mother was sitting in her chair. Normally, she was grateful for company, but she hardly stirred as we came in.

"Mother," Mary said. "We want to talk to you."

"Not about babies, I hope. That's all I've had today!"

"I'm afraid so. But it's something lovely." And crouching down by her chair, Mary told her about Gabriel's visit. Then I explained how he'd come to me too.

I needn't have worried because well before we'd finished, Mother was smiling. Then she took both our hands and asked God's blessing on us and the little one.

"Please don't tell anyone else!" I begged. "They won't understand."

"Don't worry, Joseph; your secret's safe with me. But one day, they'll all have to know."

CHAPTER FIVE

Overnight, things got even more difficult.

People started avoiding me, and I had to go across to Sepphoris to find work. Then one morning, I went to see Mother and found a neighbor talking to her.

She snorted when she saw me. "I'm surprised you've got the gall to show your face in here after the way you've behaved!" she snarled, then stalked out without giving me a chance to say anything.

"How dare she say that?" I exclaimed, but Mother just looked at me sadly.

"I'm sorry, Joseph, but I'm afraid you'll have to put up with it."

"But it's all so unfair!"

She nodded sadly. "It's like that. That's the price you pay when you obey God. I'm sure it'll work itself out, though it would be nice if I could find someone who was pleased about my future grandson!"

But things were much, much worse for Mary. All her friends had deserted her: some turned their backs when she walked by while others shouted insults.

"Little hussy!"

"Always making out she was so pure."

"We should stone her."

"Don't let the kids near her!"

Mary was a real favorite with the children. As she walked along the street, they used to appear from nowhere and rush out to her. More often than not, she'd be cuddling a toddler who'd fallen over or wiping his nose.

Now all that changed. Angry mothers shouted to their children, "Come here. Don't you go near that nasty woman!"

Once I saw her comforting a little girl and giving her some water. The child had just started drinking when her mother hurried up, snatched the cup away, and smashed it on the ground.

"Don't you dare go near her or I'll have the hide off you!"

Once when I came back at midday after a fruitless morning looking for work, I saw Mary collecting water from the well.

"What are you doing here?" I said. "It's awfully hot; why not wait till evening?"

She sighed deeply. "It's the best time to come when no one else is around."

"I didn't realize it was that bad."

"I'm afraid so. I don't know why they hate me so much. I'd give anything for someone to talk to. I feel so hot and sick, my back aches, and I'm tired all the time."

I couldn't think of anything to say, but then she smiled. "I'm sorry, Joe. I shouldn't moan. I'll be fine once I've had a bit of a rest. And I'm very lucky to have you to look after me."

"But I'm not much good."

"You are, you know." Then she blushed. "The awful thing is that a lot of men think they can do what they like to me; they reckon I'm that sort of girl. If it wasn't for you being around, things could be very difficult."

I saw what she meant when we met James.

"Got a good one for you Joe, and I fancy Mary might like it too!" And he began one of his smutty stories. I felt her stiffen and noticed she was blushing.

"James! Stop it! Not in front of Mary!"

"Oh, I thought you'd given her a rather broader view of life lately. Who knows, it might teach her a few things to brighten up your love life!"

I hit him hard. Then we rolled, fighting on the ground like boys, till some men pulled us apart. I stood up stiffly and found my nose was bleeding. Mary brushed me down while the others watched silently.

"Oh Joe!" she said when we got home. "You didn't have to do that! I think you ought to go back and apologize."

"Apologize to James after what he said? He started it—it's up to him to say sorry."

But Mary's worst disappointment was with the rabbi. They had struck up a firm friendship, and unusually, he had allowed her to join his Hebrew class as he taught the boys to read the sacred Scriptures. She proved a far better pupil than any of them and soon had memorized whole passages.

But one evening, I found her crying.

She wouldn't tell me what was wrong to start with, but at last, she said very quietly, "It's Ezra."

"Why? What's he done?"

"Well, I went round there this morning, but he ... he ... he wouldn't let me in."

"What? But I thought he was your friend? I suppose it was because of ... ?"

"Yes, because of the baby. He shouted that he didn't want to see me again, ever. And the worst thing was he did it in front of all the boys. He called me a Jezebel and said I was no better than a common prostitute. Then they all started laughing and crowding round me. I thought I was going to get hurt."

I leapt up. "I'll get him! Nobody's going to talk to my wife like that!"

She caught my sleeve. "No, Joe, you mustn't do anything! It was bad enough with James. If you have a row with Ezra, you'll have the whole village against us. Remember the baby!"

"Well, one thing's for certain! That's the last time we go to synagogue!"

"Joe, love! I know how you feel! But we've got to carry on somehow. Anyway it's not Ezra that matters; we go there to worship God."

And indeed, we went along next Sabbath and I joined the men in the hall. Mary was very quiet afterward, then Miriam explained what had happened.

"I can't help admiring that wife of yours, whatever she's done. When she got into the women's gallery, they stopped talking and turned their backs on her. She wanted to sit down on the rear bench, but then they started swearing and spitting at her and told her to get up."

"But she's near her time. It's very tiring for her to stand."

"That didn't seem to worry them, but I did manage to make a space for her. We got some filthy looks and some pretty unpleasant comments, but who cares?"

Looking back, I realize that as the weeks went by, I must have grown increasingly difficult to live with. All the snubs and unkindnesses were getting to me, and I was becoming very depressed.

"It's so unfair!" I kept telling myself. "I get married and I can't even sleep with my wife—I've waited long enough in all conscience! It's Mary's baby, and I'm getting blamed for it! The whole village treats us like dirt and I'm beginning to wish I'd never heard of Messiah!"

By contrast, Mary was growing more peaceful. If I'd had to put up with her problems, I'd have had flaming rows every day, but she was so calm, carrying on as if nothing had happened and singing psalms to herself.

I remember one evening about a month before the baby was due. I came in after work, and there she was sitting in the corner. She got up, though it was clearly an effort, and gave me her special smile. Her voice was low. "Joe. You don't have to go through with this if you don't want to."

I stared at her. "What are you talking about?"

"Look, I know you're finding it rough. Wouldn't it be better to divorce me? Then you can find a nice girl and have your own family."

I looked at her, horrified. "Mary, don't you love me anymore?"

"Of course I do! But I've been thinking it's not right to drag you through all this."

"But what would you do if we split up? I mean, where would you go? Who'd look after you? What about the baby?"

This wasn't what I meant to say: I wanted to tell her how much I loved her, but the words didn't come out somehow.

"I'll manage all right. I've got to. Women can't run away from these things."

"But I can't let you go! It's not right!"

"Look, Joe, it's not right to ask you to put up with it. Not the way things are now."

I didn't know what to say, but she must have seen the tears in my eyes because she added, "Oh Joe, I'm so sorry! I'm saying all the wrong things."

"No, you're not."

"Well ... You see, I've promised God I'll have the baby and I know he's going to look after me. Remember how it all worked out when I went down to meet Elizabeth?"

"But it's so hard for you!"

She paused a bit; then she beamed. "Joe, it's the most marvelous thing that ever happened to a woman! I don't know why God picked me, but it's going to be wonderful having Jesus."

"But Mary, don't you realize? I'm not backing out either. I'm in it just as much as you are. I mean, I saw the angel too, and I promised God I'd make you my wife and love you and your child!"

And then she started crying and I had the sense to put my arm round her.

A bit later, I started again. "But it's so unfair. We get blamed for having sex before we got married, but it's never happened! We try to do things right and everybody hates us!"

She nodded. "It does seem like that. But I know the old prophets felt the same way. Whenever they tried to tell people what God was saying, everyone turned on them."

"But we haven't deserved it!"

"We haven't deserved God's blessing either. An awful lot of women would think it unfair that I should bear Messiah, and a lot of men would envy you."

"What do you mean envy me?"

"Joe, you've got a marvelous opportunity. Jesus will look up to you as father. He'll watch the things you do and copy you. It'll be difficult enough for him growing up, and he'll need all the support and love you can give him."

"I suppose it'll work out all right?"

"Well, he'll find it hard; children can be very cruel. Once they know he was conceived before we got married, they're sure to call him a bastard. That's why we've got to stand together and give him all the support we can."

"I'm trying my best."

"But Joe, it's not just that. What sort of life will it be if we aren't on speaking terms with anyone in the village?"

She was right, of course. I felt a fool, but that evening I went round to sort things out with James. His wife, Susannah, opened the door and looked very surprised to see me, while James seemed embarrassed. I think he was feeling rather silly too. But anyway, we had a drink together and things were better after that.

CHAPTER SIX

The census gave us a fresh start.

Not that it seemed a good idea at the time; I was horrified it'd take me away from Mary just when she needed me most.

There'd been rumors for some days, but Ezra made the formal announcement one Sabbath in synagogue. We were all set to leave when he cleared his throat and started in that pompous way of his.

"May I have your attention? I have an important communication from the Roman authorities, which I will now read to you."

There were some whistles and catcalls; we're a pretty independent lot in Galilee.

"Silence, please! I wish to draw your attention to the fact that I am commanded to make a proclamation. The sooner I can complete this task the better for all concerned."

"Why's he got to tell us?" I muttered to my brother Simon. "Can't the Romans do their own dirty work?"

"I guess they prefer to leave it to the locals. That way there's less chance of a riot."

Ezra was still trying to make himself heard. At last, there was a sullen silence. Then he started speaking in Greek.

"By order of the Emperor Caesar Augustus, our noble King Herod and Quirinius, Governor of Syria ..."

I'll spare you the details, all their special titles and things. We use Greek in the market, but this was official stuff full of long words, and I didn't pay much attention.

I wasn't the only one. When he'd done, James shouted out, "What's all that rubbish mean?"

Ezra looked furious. "I would have thought it would be obvious if you had had the courtesy to listen. The authorities have decided to hold a census to enable them to make the collection of taxes more equitable ..."

"So they can grab more money!" someone yelled. Then there was fresh uproar.

Ezra stood waving his arms till the noise died down. "I am not prepared to spend my time struggling to make myself heard. If you wish to know what I have to say, you must be quiet!"

Simon's voice boomed out. "Shut up, the lot of you!"

Ezra straightened his robe. "The Romans require a full list of adult men to enable them to set a fair level of taxes. As a consequence, every male must report to his ancestral home so that he may be counted."

"But why can't we do it here?"

"Because in their wisdom the authorities have decreed otherwise!"

We filed out still grumbling.

"But I still don't see why we can't be counted in the village," I complained to James.

"That would be far too easy. They enjoy making things difficult."

"But you don't have far to go, have you?"

"No, I'm lucky. My family's originally from Capernaum. But yours was from Judea, wasn't it?"

"That's right—more's the pity. Bethlehem, just beyond Jerusalem. I only hope I can delay till Mary's had the baby."

"I suppose you'll be away some time."

"Knowing the Romans, it could be at least two weeks and that'll be too long."

Just then I saw Ezra coming out, so I went to have a word with him. "Excuse me, sir, but must I attend this census immediately? I don't want to leave my wife at the moment since her baby's due any day."

He shrugged. "The order is quite clear. You are required to be registered by the end of next month at the very latest; there are no exceptions. All I can suggest is that you pray your wife will have her offspring before you leave."

"But that's not fair! I've got to go all the way to Judea!"

He laughed. "If you had thought first before your eh ... fornication, you would not have had this problem!"

I was still fuming when I caught up with Mary.

"I'd like to push his face in! He doesn't have to leave a pregnant woman while he heads off to the other end of the country! I only asked if I could delay a bit, but he wouldn't listen."

But to my surprise, she seemed excited. "Isn't it Bethlehem you're going to?"

"Yes, I'm afraid so."

"Oh that's wonderful!"

I stared at her. "What do you mean wonderful?"

"Don't you remember? That's where the prophet said Messiah's going to be born."

"I didn't know that."

"Oh yes, I checked up with Ezra before he turned nasty. So if I come with you, I can have the baby in the right town."

"But you can't travel like this! You might give birth at any time."

"If God wants Messiah born in Bethlehem, he'll look after me and the child till we get there. Anyway, I don't want to be left behind here with everyone being so nasty." Then she smiled. "It's nice of the Romans to make the arrangements for me!"

Simon called in that evening. "I don't know if you've made any plans, but I hear there's a party going down to Jerusalem, and Bethlehem's just a short step from there."

"That sounds good. Mary and I would love to join them if they'll have us."

"What? You're not taking Mary? You must be joking!"

"But she wants to come."

"That's crazy! She doesn't have to be registered, and the last thing she needs right now is a long journey."

"The last thing she needs right now is to be left alone in this village with the way folks are treating her. However rough the journey, she'll be better off with me. And I expect you'll be coming with us?"

He looked a little embarrassed. "Eh … no … I have a few things to deal with here first, so I'll be down later. I expect we'll meet up there."

"And who's leading this trip you mentioned?"

"Isaac. You know, the potter from down the village."

My heart sank. I hadn't liked him even when we were boys together, and these last few months, he'd cut me dead. But it looked as if I'd have to speak to him.

He wasn't pleased to see me either, particularly when I said that Mary was coming as well. "Look, Joe, I'm warning you now. We're not going to be hanging around. Keep up or you'll get left behind. And if your woman does go into labor, you'll be on your own."

"Don't worry; we'll do our best."

"Mind you do!"

Normally Mary would have walked, but I could hardly expect her to do so this time. I had an old donkey, but I didn't think it was up to the trip, so I had to buy another for her to ride, though that one didn't look much better. I loaded it with food and a bag of tools. If I was lucky, I might pick up some work while we were waiting. I could use the money.

Then it was time to go. Mary's parents seemed glad to be rid of us, but my mother stood to say goodbye although she'd been feeling quite unwell recently, and she was hanging onto the doorpost with one hand and raising the other in blessing.

"Joe, be sure you look after Mary and the precious one God's given her."

I looked back as we came to a bend in the path. She was still standing and waving, though with her weak eyes, I doubt she could see us.

We found Isaac pacing up and down. "Joe, I told you to get here early. The others are well on their way by now!"

We hurried over the hill to Sepphoris. "I hope we'll catch them up in town," I remarked. "With any luck, they'll be buying stuff for the journey." And to my relief they were still there.

Our route would take us along the Jordan Valley before the final long climb to Jerusalem. There's a shorter way through Samaria, but our religious leaders tell us to keep clear of the folks there since they're heretics.

We followed the main road as far as the Sea of Galilee. I've lost count of the times I've been that way, but I still catch my breath every time I come over the hill and see the blue water far below. And on a clear day, there's Mount Hermon with its snow at the head of the great valley.

The road descended in a series of sharp bends. There was one anxious moment when the donkey slipped, but we managed to get down safely. There I saw several fishing boats pulled up on the shore, reminding me of a time I'd spent working in Capernaum.

"I'd love some fresh fish," Mary said. "It's so much better than that dried stuff we get at home." But there was no time to stop; Isaac was hurrying the folk on as he wanted to go as far as possible before sundown.

We pushed on past a large graveyard and some hot springs. They'd built a lot of bathhouses there recently, and it was very popular with the Romans. Then we came to the marshes where the river flows out of the lake.

I don't like the Jordan Valley. It's too hot for me and I dread to think how Mary felt with the baby due. The river twists and turns as if it's uncomfortable too, and most of the time you can't see the water for trees. "Watch out!" Mary warned. "Once when I was little, I saw a lion coming out of a thicket near here!"

The caravanserai was full up, so we camped in the open with the men taking turns to keep watch. It wasn't cold, but the ground was hard, and although I made a bed for Mary, she didn't get much sleep. The water wasn't much good either, but we bought some dates, which helped hide the salty flavor.

We pushed on down the valley for two more days. We had odd glimpses of the hills, which became very bare as we headed south, and through gaps in the trees, we could see the land just beyond us was desert.

"Another day should see us there," I said as we stopped for the night near Jericho.

"Oh I hope so!" Mary replied. "I keep praying the baby won't come till we get to Bethlehem."

I looked at her, slightly alarmed. "Do you think it might?"

"I'm getting the odd pain now and then."

One of the few women in our party was Joanna, who delivered most of the babies back home, so I went to find her. "Could you please have a look at Mary? She may be starting the baby."

"I don't know as I should really. Not after the way she's behaved. But find me a lamp; I'll do my best."

I waited nervously while she made her examination. "Well, she's not in labor yet, though I reckon it won't be long. But being a first one, you can't be sure."

"Is it safe for us to carry on?"

She frowned. "If it were up to me, I'd stay in Jericho and have the child there. But she seems fair set on getting to Bethlehem."

"Of course. I have to go there to register."

"Yes maybe you do. But it's not right to take her along too—it's not right at all! What that girl needs is peace and quiet, not bouncing around on top of a donkey!"

"I'll make her rest once we get there."

"It may be too late by then!" Then she gave me an odd look. "Funny that. When I looked at her just now, I'd have sworn she was a virgin if it hadn't been for the baby. I just don't know how you two managed it!"

CHAPTER SEVEN

Next morning, Isaac sounded worried. "Now listen all of you! Today we've got to keep together; this is the worst bit of the journey. Last month, ten men got robbed by bandits round here."

Then he glared at me. "I don't want any lagging behind. We must be up that hill well before sundown so we can get into Jerusalem before they shut the gates."

Sure enough, it was our worst day: one long climb, no shade or green anywhere, and the goats we saw seemed to be eating rock. Even the hills looked odd, sharp points instead of curves. The only good thing was we didn't see any robbers.

But it was almost sundown before we reached Bethany, a little short of the city. Isaac was annoyed. "I told you to hurry! We should have been in town by now instead of being stuck out here for the night!"

I hardly dared look at Mary, but once she'd had a drink of water, she perked up. "Joe, I'm glad we didn't make Bethlehem tonight. It'll be easier tomorrow; we should be there well before midday, and that'll give us a chance to find somewhere to stay."

"How are you feeling?"

"A lot better, thanks. Now what are we going to eat tonight? And have you got any fodder for the donkey?"

I tried to get her to lie down, but she insisted on sorting out our baggage and checking we had enough rags for when the baby came.

Next morning, Isaac was a little calmer. "Right, Joe. This is where you leave us. There's a couple of families going down to Bethlehem, but you better keep your eyes open for trouble."

"When are you going back home?"

"Depends on how long the census takes. But I hope to be coming through here a week today, pretty early in the morning. If you're not around then, you'll have to find your own way back."

"Well, thanks for all your help."

He nodded and turned to someone else.

We went off along a narrow track. After a bit, the others started complaining we were holding them back.

"I'm sorry," I said. "This donkey's tired out, and I'm getting the best pace out of her I can."

Then one of the men pointed out a pile of stones. "See that, Joe? That's where Rachel died."

"You mean Jacob's wife?"

"That's right. His favorite. She was having a baby, Benjamin as I recall. They saved him all right, but they couldn't do anything for her." Then he chuckled. "Hope you have better luck with your missus!"

I'd never heard a stupider remark. What a thing to remind Mary of! I took a quick look at her, but she didn't seem to have heard. She'd been quite lively when we started off, but now her eyes were closed and her knuckles were white where she was clutching the donkey's saddle.

"How much longer will it be, Joe? I'm beginning to feel really uncomfortable."

The others had gone on ahead. I ran after them and asked how much further they thought it would be.

"We're nearly there," one woman shrugged.

We made it eventually. I'd been to Bethlehem once or twice before and thought it a pretty sleepy place. But today there were people and animals milling round everywhere, and it was as much as we could do to force our way down the street.

"Anywhere we can put up for the night?" I shouted to one man as he shouldered his way past.

"Some hope!" he laughed. "There are folks here who've been sleeping rough for a week."

"Where's the inn then?"

He jerked his thumb at a doorway. "You're right by it! Only I wouldn't waste your time going in; it's jammed solid!"

I found somewhere to hitch the donkey and left Mary sitting on it. I had to wriggle my way in through the crowd and clamber over piles of bedding. Eventually, I spotted the innkeeper, a middle-aged man running round frantically.

It took time to attract his attention, but I was desperate. "Look," I shouted. "My wife's having a baby in the street! She needs somewhere to lie down!"

He raised his hands in despair. "God give me strength! So am I the wickedest man in Bethlehem that he doesn't give me space to lie down and then sends me a woman in labor who wants a bed?"

He rubbed sweat off his brow with a hairy arm. Then suddenly, he grabbed me and shouted, "Come on!"

I'm big, but he manhandled me out of there like a child, barging a few paces down the street and then pointing to a hole in the wall. "That's it!" he yelled. "Take it or leave it." Then he was fighting his way back into the inn.

It was a stable. Some rough bits of wood had been fixed across the opening, but I could just see some cows inside. I stared in horror while Mary cried out again. I'd never been closer to panic.

Then I realized a woman was trying to talk to me.

"Don't you mind that innkeeper! That's my husband, Tom. Don't mean no harm, but he's rushed off his feet. We ain't known nothing like this, what with this wretched census!"

Before I could say anything, she turned to Mary. "First one, is it, love? Mind if I have a look? I'm Hannah; I do all the babies round here. Sort you out in no time."

I couldn't believe our luck. I might be a country boy and I've helped with lambing often enough, but I didn't want to tackle this, particularly since I knew who the baby was.

She patted my arm. "Don't worry, love! Just leave it to me. But we better get her in there fast; we ain't got much time."

I undid the bars. It smelt terrible inside and the floor was filthy; it couldn't have been mucked out for months. It was only a cave, but it did go back quite a way and I saw what I hoped was a pile of clean straw against the far wall.

I got Mary inside, and she leant against me while Hannah made a bed from straw. Then she straightened up. "Wait! I'll be right back. I need a lamp—I've got one at home we can use. Hey, by the way, what are your names?"

"This is Mary, and I'm Joe."

"Right, Joe. The first thing you've got to do is get that donkey in here or it'll go for a walk with all these strangers around! Then tie those ruddy cows up, or they'll be right in the way."

I brought the donkey inside and unloaded it. I had just finished with the cows when Hannah came back with the lamp and an empty pitcher.

"Now Joe, we need water. I'm afraid you'll have to fill this up. The well's just along there by the gate."

This was women's work, and I felt embarrassed waiting my turn to draw water. Somehow the girls manage to balance a full pitcher on a shoulder, but I had to lug it back the best way I could.

Hannah was coming out of the stable. "Ah good! There you are! She should be all right for a moment. I'm just going to get some more stuff. Can you find something for the baby to sleep in?"

I gave Mary a drink of water, then found an old manger propped up against the wall. It was pretty dirty, but I took one of our rags and cleaned it out. Once I'd filled it with straw and covered it with a cloth, it didn't look too bad.

Hannah came back carrying a big bundle. She was none too soon; everything was beginning to happen. I could hardly bear to watch; instead, I noticed the way the cows strained on their ropes to get as close a view as possible. Then there was the dreadful moment when Mary began crying out.

Suddenly, it was all over. Hannah was holding a baby, who was wailing loudly.

"Congratulations, Joe! You've got a fine boy!"

In a moment, she'd tied off the cord. Then she pushed a bowl toward me. "Stick some water in that."

I fumbled with the pitcher and accidentally slopped some over her feet. "Take it easy," she grinned. "It's him as needs the water not me!"

In no time, she'd wiped him over with a wet cloth and dried him. She put him down for a moment as she dug in her bag then rubbed him over with salt and wrapped a rag round him.

"Here Joe! You hold on to him while I finish up here. Sorry he's a bit messy, but I've never done one in a stable before!"

I was scared I'd drop him. I've picked up my sisters' children often enough, but he was much lighter. I couldn't see much in the lamplight, just a screwed-up face and some dark hair. Of course, it would have been different if he'd been my own child, but this was like holding a stranger's.

It was funny, really; we'd talked often enough about him being Messiah, but I hadn't thought what he'd look like. I suppose I fancied he would be rather more impressive than this!

Then something I'd heard in synagogue came back to me. I think it came from the prophet Isaiah, "He didn't have any beauty or majesty to attract us to him, there was nothing in his appearance to make us desire him." I think that referred to Messiah, but anyway Mary would know.

Hannah was really getting on with it. In next to no time, she'd sorted Mary out and bundled the spare rags together. Then she took the baby from me and gave him to his mother, moving the lamp round so she could see. There was a lovely smile on her face as she lay there with the child.

"I best be off in a moment," Hannah said. "Sorry to leave you to it, but I need to wash before sundown to get rid of my impurity after doing all this. I've got to give Tom a hand—he'll be in a fair state without me!"

"We're really sorry to put you to all this trouble."

"Don't worry, it's been a pleasure! And if you need anything, you know where I am." Then she pointed her finger at me. "And don't forget, Joe, you're unclean too what with handling the baby and stuff. Don't touch anybody else if you can help it till you've had a wash. Got anything to wrap the baby in?"

"Yes, we brought some bands with us."

"Good. Give 'em here."

I took the bandages from our pack, and in a moment, she had wrapped the baby up with his arms held down by his side.

"Thank you so much," Mary said weakly. "I just don't know how we'd have coped without you."

"Oh that's nothing! By the way, have you got some oil? You'll need to put some on him three times a day, and I've got some powdered myrtle leaves to rub in as well if you haven't got any. My mother used to swear by that."

Now I was coming to the awkward moment. "How much do we owe you?"

She snorted. "Nothing at all, love! If I can't help some of David's family, things are in a pretty bad way! Anyway, it looks like you haven't got two shekels to rub together."

Then after a last glance round, she was gone with an armful of dirty rags.

I gave Mary another drink and some of the dates that were left over, but she didn't fancy anything else. She fed the baby, then put him down in the manger.

I was feeling quite hungry, so after I'd had a wash, I ate some bread with dried fish and figs. I had quite a surprise when I looked outside. It was dark already, so I topped up Hannah's lamp and lay down next to Mary to get some sleep.

CHAPTER EIGHT

I couldn't get to sleep; there was too much on my mind.

Back home, I could have gone outside for a walk. But I wouldn't risk it here; I might get a spear stuck in me by a suspicious soldier. Anyway, I couldn't leave Mary with the new baby.

If only I had someone to chat to! There were a lot of folk outside, but they were all strangers with their own problems: what was one more child to them? I would have given anything to see friendly faces like some of my mates once they'd got over their snide remarks, we'd have made quite a night of it, wetting the baby's head and putting the world to rights!

Then I thought of my brother Simon. He'd been very helpful finding us a group to travel with, but why hadn't he joined us? Did he really have a pressing reason to come later, or was he ashamed of us like everyone else? Wasn't there anyone apart from Mother who was pleased to see us?

If it came down to it, I'd have even settled for my cousin Reuben. He's not the sort of bloke you can have a serious conversation with, but he's always good for a laugh, and that's why I chose him as my chief companion for the wedding. But he'd gone to Capernaum, where his family came from, so I didn't expect to see him till this was all over.

Originally, I'd planned such a different life for Mary and myself. She'd have had her babies in the comfort of her own home, not in a filthy stable like this! It should have been the happiest time of our lives, but there'd been one thing after another these last few months, and being stuck in this filthy hole was the end! Fancy having to have a baby in here! If only I'd insisted on stopping off in Bethany or I'd argued with that innkeeper till we got somewhere decent!

I could imagine Mary's parents glowering at me, and I started making excuses. "Yes, I know you think I've let her down, making her have her baby in here, but it's not my fault! I haven't any money, and anyway, everywhere is crowded out—blame the Romans for that! And she insisted on coming along too. If you'd been nicer to her, maybe she'd have stayed put in Nazareth! And the baby's not my fault either whatever you think!"

I paused. "I suppose things could have been worse. At least Mary and the baby are safe, and I can thank God for Hannah. If she hadn't turned up like that ... well, it doesn't bear thinking about!"

I could just see Mary in the lamplight, sleeping peacefully with the improvised cradle beside her. Suddenly I longed to cuddle her and was reaching over when a voice in my head stopped me. "Leave her alone, Joe! She's dead tired. She needs all the sleep she can get without you bothering her!"

I started talking to Mary, quietly so as not to rouse her. "I'm sorry, love. I've tried to do what I could for you. Though I say it myself, our new place in Nazareth isn't bad; there's plenty of girls who would put up with worse than that! And I even let you go off to see Elizabeth instead of getting married earlier!"

I stopped myself. "No! That's not true. I didn't give you permission. You insisted on going, and there wasn't anything I could do about it! And I was mean and spiteful like a spoilt kid! And when you came back ..."

I could hardly bear to think about that night even now. It niggled away at me like a sore tooth. I'd never forget how she'd looked at me.

I shook myself. "Don't be silly, Joe! It's all finished! I said sorry. I've done my best to make it up to her. I hope she understood. She said she'd forgiven me."

But then I'm ashamed to say the old fear came back: did Mary tell me the truth about the baby?

I gritted my teeth. "Stop it, Joe! You've been through all this before! You saw Gabriel, didn't you? He told you what happened, how God gave her this baby. What more proof do you need?"

I could still remember the joy I'd felt after he'd gone and the sheer relief. I'd give anything to feel like that again, but it seems like it happened to someone else a long time ago. Perhaps it was a dream after all and I imagined the whole thing.

I was sweating. "Whose kid was it then? I'd swallowed her story, but it took some believing! She must have cheated on me, and what would my mates think if they knew? Or maybe one of them was the father."

This was madness. "Stop it, Joe! Stop it!" I gasped.

But the doubts kept coming. "How about that visit to Elizabeth? Was it just a story to put me off? Perhaps she never went near the place but met a lover elsewhere! That was nine months ago; it fits very nicely!"

I clenched my fists till they hurt. "Some marriage I've got! Thanks to her I've lost my friends and driven Mother mad. Even my in-laws treat me as a scoundrel!"

I looked at Mary once again, but she was sleeping as quietly as ever. "It's all right for you! Enjoy your little romance about Messiah; if God ever sends him, he won't choose us as parents!"

I could just see the baby's head in the manger. "Poor kid! What sort of life will he have? Like his mum said, they'll call him a bastard! Some Messiah he'd be! Why didn't God make sure he was born in a palace instead of on a pile of muck?"

Then suddenly I felt angry. The whole thing was a mess. If it weren't for this, I would still enjoy a place in village life instead of being treated like an outcast! The baby might be tiny, but he'd wrecked our lives. I could almost hate him—a young cuckoo in our nest!

Then the tears started running down my cheeks, but I tried not to make any noise. My doubts would have to be my secret; I'd never let Mary know how I felt!

It was quiet outside, just the sound of wind rustling the leaves; then I heard a noise. Men were coming down the street. They sounded excited, talking and singing.

"Sounds like they've had a jar or two!" I thought. "I hope they don't bother us!"

I expected them to carry on down the road, but instead they stopped a short way up. I sidled over to the doorway and in the moonlight saw them standing outside the inn. One held a torch and another was banging on the door, shouting for the landlord. He made such a racket I thought he would wake Mary and the baby.

Then there was a roar from inside and a string of oaths followed by crashes as the locking bars were ripped away. Then Tom stood filling the doorway with his bulk. He was blazing mad.

"What do you think you're doing? Can't you let a body sleep? Any more noise and I'll set Herod's men on you!"

I'll say this for the man who'd been knocking. He stood his ground even though the landlord was twice his size.

"We've come to find the king."

I've never seen a man so dumbfounded. It took him quite a time to find his tongue. Then he screamed.

"King! Here? You're bloody mad! You stupid halfwit! I've never heard such rubbish! Waking me up in the middle of the night to find a king!"

"Well, you see, an angel told us he'd be here!"

I thought Tom would have a fit. His eyes bulged, and even in that light, I could see him going purple. "An angel told you ..."

"That's right! He said that this king's been born here tonight and we'd find him lying in a manger. Then we saw a whole lot more angels! They lit the whole sky up!"

Suddenly Tom leapt forward and grabbed him by the throat. I thought he'd kill him on the spot, but instead he marched him over toward our cave.

"A baby? A bloody baby you want? Right, you can have one! Born here tonight! Right in the muck where you belong. Get in there and find your king! But I'm telling you, one more cheep out of you and I'll have you strung up if it's the last thing I do!"

He threw the man against the wall then whirled round. The street echoed as the inn door crashed shut and the locking bars were slammed into place.

The man must have received quite a bang as he stood there for some time holding his head. Then he whispered something to the others before coming across and tapping gently on one of the boards across the cave's entrance.

"Is anyone there?" His voice was more nervous now.

"Yes. Hang on a moment; I'm coming."

I went back and pulled on my tunic and picked up the lamp. I edged my way out, trying to avoid the worst of the dung. Just as I got to the opening, I realized I'd forgotten to bring a stick with me. I hoped they wouldn't turn nasty.

I could see them properly now, six men in shaggy robes, workmen of some kind by the look of them.

"What do you want?" I whispered. "My wife's in here and she's just had a baby. For goodness sake, keep quiet; they're asleep."

"Sir," the man said. "I think that baby's the one we've come to see!"

"But you can't come in! My wife's only just given birth, and I've never seen you before!"

"No sir. We're just shepherds, and we're very sorry to bother you so late. But you see, sir, an angel told us to come."

They looked very shy, shifting from one foot to the other, but for all that, they were very excited. It reminded me of how I'd felt after Gabriel's visit. Then I started smiling. The look of relief on their faces was almost comical.

"Yes, of course, you can come in and see him. But I better warn my wife."

Mary opened her eyes as I walked over. "Who were you talking to just now?"

"You won't believe this! But there're some shepherds outside who say they've seen an angel. They say he sent them here to find a king that's just been born ..."

She didn't let me finish. "Joe! They've come to see Jesus!"

CHAPTER NINE

She sat up, pulling her robe round her and pushing her hair back off her forehead. The men trooped in shyly and looked nervously at her before gathering round the manger staring at the baby like they'd never seen one before.

The man who'd done all the talking whispered, "It's him right enough." And to my surprise, they got down on the floor and lay flat in the muck like they were on a carpet. Then they started crying out.

"Thank you, Lord ... It's him ... Never thought I'd see him ... Messiah come at last ... What a baby ... Isn't he marvelous ..."

I'm used to Ezra praying every Sabbath at synagogue. He goes on and on and I usually have a doze while he's doing it, but these were real prayers.

Most shepherds don't say much what with only sheep to talk to, but these men were really excited and their words just poured out. Sometimes they'd lift their heads to take another peep at Jesus, but then they'd lie down again and keep praising God.

I felt an outsider. There was Mary, smiling at the baby asleep in the manger, and all around were those strangers worshipping him. And I was just watching, ashamed of the thoughts I'd just had.

It made me think that these men had seen an angel and came straight down here. I'd seen an angel too, but when the child was born, instead of praising God, I'd felt sorry for myself.

But then something wonderful happened. Suddenly, incredibly, I felt God was standing next to me and I was filled with wonder. I got down on the ground with the shepherds and started praising him.

And I began to feel quite different about Jesus.

So far, although I had tried to do my best to obey what the angel told me, the baby had just seemed an inconvenience. He was just another child who had been passed to me to look after. But now I realized he really was my own son, as if I'd sired him myself. Our law said as much: if I adopted him, he'd be counted as my own flesh and blood. He wouldn't come between me and Mary, but in fact, he was the most wonderful gift we could have.

Somewhere in the Scriptures, it talks about a son being born to us who'd be the Prince of Peace and the Mighty God. I didn't rightly know what that meant, but I thought it must refer somehow to Jesus, and it made me so excited I thought my chest would burst.

I don't know how long this went on for, but then Jesus woke and started crying. Mary picked him up and, turning her back on our guests, started feeding him.

We stood up, and the man who'd spoken hugged me. "Thank you, sir; we thank you most gratefully for letting us see him. It's been the best day of our lives!"

I felt lost for words. "Well ... eh .... Thank you very much for coming. You've been such an encouragement to us."

Then Mary spoke. "It's been wonderful to see you and a huge joy to us."

The shepherds shuffled their feet. "Best be getting along now. Must see how the sheep are."

They all bowed to the baby, then groped their way outside. I watched them walking up the street singing praises to God, and several doors opened as folk came out to see what the noise was.

Then I remembered Ezra saying that they don't accept a shepherd's testimony in a court of law. Normally, those who do that job are boys or folk who're weak in the head and no one takes much notice of them. How strange then that God sent his angel to them rather than more important folk! Mind you, my ancestor King David started out as a shepherd on these same hills, and I doubt I'd have spotted the difference if he'd come along tonight!

I waited till I couldn't hear them anymore. When I got back to Mary, she was still holding Jesus, and I caught my breath as I saw her; she was so beautiful. She had a slight smile and seemed to be gazing miles away as she sang a lullaby.

The baby's eyes were very heavy, and he was soon asleep. She put him down gently, then smiled at me.

"Wasn't it wonderful the way those men came?"

I nodded.

Then she said, "You know, as I've been sitting here, I've been thinking how very kind God was to cheer us up like that. I was feeling a bit down before they came, and their visit was just what I needed."

I looked at her in surprise. "You felt a bit down? But you always seem so happy."

"Well, I try to be and obviously it's special being a mum, but things have been a bit difficult recently. It would have been so nice if he'd been born in a comfortable place with your mother to help."

"I'm sorry; I should have done better for you," I muttered.

"You've done very well, Joe. You've brought me to the right town and found me somewhere to have the baby. It's just that ... well, I know it sounds silly, but I wanted you to hold my hand."

I reached out to her and we sat together looking at Jesus. It was on the tip of my tongue to tell her how I'd been feeling before the shepherds came, but I didn't think it right to burden her with all that. Still I think she guessed.

"I know you feel cheated about the baby. It must be awful to know he's not yours. But in a funny way, I don't feel he belongs to me either. He's been lent to us, and we've both got to learn to love him and treat him like our own."

I made myself a bed and slept well despite the excitement. It was light when I opened my eyes and saw Mary feeding Jesus. Now I could get a proper look at him: he was a handsome little chap and sucking lustily.

After a bit, she put him up against her shoulder and rubbed his back. She smiled up at me a bit shyly.

"Bringing up his wind! I've done this a few times with my sisters' babies, but it's nice to have one of my own!"

He belched and she smiled, patting him gently. "Good boy! Bring it all up!"

Then she looked at me. "Want to take him for a bit?"

She held the bundle out. "Don't be frightened; just make sure you support his head properly!"

Once more, I was surprised at how light he was, wondering how anything this small could grow into a big man.

"Joe. Give his back another rub. Gently!"

I started rubbing, and suddenly he puked and a spurt of milk went onto my shoulder. She laughed.

"Wait a moment; I'll wipe it off for you! I'm afraid you'll have to get used to that!"

I grinned. "Mother always reckons that when they're that age, all they do is feed, sleep, and mess themselves!"

"I think that's about right! Shall I take him again?"

I shook my head; I was enjoying myself. Then I remembered something else I'd been told: one of the most amazing things about a baby is its fingernails.

He had made a fist of his hand, but I prized it open gently. He had pink nails, each one tiny but quite perfect. But then I smelt something unpleasant, so I gave him back to Mary, who wrinkled her nose. "I think I'd better change you, my boy!"

Soon he was lying asleep in the manger, and she looked around her. "My! Everything's in a mess. I'd better tidy it up!"

"Can't you leave it? I don't want you getting tired."

"Oh I feel fine now. Wait till we've got six children and a baby!"

Just then, we heard a gentle tap. A wizened old man was peering in nervously, and behind him was a youth. They were carrying shepherd's crooks.

"Have you come to see the baby?" Mary asked.

"Well, yes please." It was the young man who spoke. "If we might, that is. You see, our mates came down here last night, but we had to stay back to mind the sheep."

They looked at Jesus for a bit, then they too lay down by the manger and worshipped. And I shared their joy and wonder.

At last, they raised their heads, and the old man's face softened. I could guess how gentle he'd be with an orphan lamb.

"So what did happen last night?" I asked. "I know you saw an angel, but I didn't get the full story."

The youth answered. "I better tell you; he can't speak. It was just an ordinary sort of night, really. We'd put all the sheep in a pen like we always do and old Judah here settled himself across the entrance. We takes it in turns, you know, to keep guard."

"I suppose you're worried about bears?"

"Yes, there's a few of them about. But it's folks mostly, them as fancies a mutton supper! Anyways, the rest of us was sitting by the fire. Then, well ..."

"You saw the angel?" I broke in.

"Not straight off, we didn't. First the sky lit up like it was midday. We all reckoned it was the end of the world. There we was on the ground, begging God for mercy and hoping we'd done enough good things to see us through! And ..."

"And then you saw the angel?"

His eyes gleamed. "That's right ... My! He was huge! Bigger than any bloke I've set eyes on! I was scared out of my wits. But then ... I dunno, he sort of calmed us down pretty quick."

I smiled, remembering Gabriel's visit. "But what then?"

"He told us he had some marvelous news for us. For us shepherds, mark you! And for everybody else too, down in David's town—that's here in Bethlehem."

I nodded.

"Well, in David's town, someone special had been born who's going to save his people. Messiah no less, the one we've been looking for. And he's going to be Lord."

He looked over his shoulder and spoke more quietly. "Not like that Herod that's king round these parts!"

"But how did you guess it was our baby?"

"I was coming to that. He told us we'd find him all wrapped up in cloth, just like any other kid, only he'd be lying in a manger. You don't see that too often, for all that we folks haven't much silver to rub together."

"But didn't you think it odd? Him being Messiah?"

He looked me straight in the eye. "I knows what I've seen and I knows what I've heard. When one of them angels talks to you, you don't argue. Anyways, it must have been him; our men found him, didn't they?"

"Oh yes, and it really cheered us up."

He smiled. "They got cheered too—and of course us today! Anyways, going back to last night, if one angel weren't enough, then we sees hundreds of them, flying everywhere, singing marvelous songs, real joyful like!"

"Did you hear the words?"

"Praise to God mostly; you know, glorifying him up in heaven and saying that we'd have peace down here, well, for all the men God had blessed. I reckon we could do with a bit of that right now what with them Romans and Herod's men!"

"It must have been amazing!"

"Never seen nothing like it, and I was wondering what they'd do next when they vanished just like that. The sky went black, and it was just us and the sheep."

"Then your friends came down here?"

"Right away. They were that excited they couldn't wait. Only me being the youngest, I had to stay behind to keep old Judah company and make sure the sheep were safe."

There was just one thing that puzzled me. "But how did they get into the town at that time of night with the gate shut?"

He chuckled. "It's not so hard when you knows how! There's a fair number of holes in that wall if you knows where to look!"

He turned to go, but the old man wasn't ready. He was twisting something in his hands; then suddenly he pushed it into mine.

The young man smiled. "Something for the baby! From all of us."

Before I could say anything, they were out of the door. I was left holding two lamb skins.

"Look at this, Mary! See what they've given us. I feel bad about taking it. They're poorer than us!"

"They wanted him to have something. It's the best present of all; he'll be really comfy on that."

CHAPTER TEN

Tom turned up soon after. He was very angry.

"Still here, then? Not got your bloody visitors with you, I hope! I could have killed them last night! Knocking my ruddy door down just when I'd got off to sleep."

He pushed inside. "Made yourself at home, I see. Your donkey looks pretty comfortable; hope he's not eating too much of my hay. And you've tied up my cows—if you've mucked them around, I'll be after you ... And that manger; when you're done, I want it back up against the wall where you found it."

"Sir. We're being very careful. And we're so grateful to you."

He snorted. "I must've been out of my mind letting you in. And you kept Hannah down here most of yesterday with me up to my eyes with the customers."

"But I ..."

"Look! I want you out of here! Now!"

"Yes, sir! We'll go just as soon as we can. Once we're registered, we'll be off home."

"I want you out before that! They're taking weeks to deal with everyone!"

"But where can we go?"

"That's your problem!"

He'd just stumped off when Hannah bustled in; she was smiling. "Was he nasty to you, then? I saw him leaving."

"He's ordered us out!"

"All in good time. Don't worry; he'll calm down once I talk to him!" Then she turned to Mary. "So how's you this morning, love? You don't look too bad. And the baby? Isn't he lovely?"

I left them to it and went for a walk. Hannah was just coming out as I got back.

"You're a lucky man, Joe! Got yourself a pretty wife and a fine boy! Mind you look after them."

"I'm doing my best."

"And excuse me asking, but where are you going to stay when you leave here?"

"I haven't found anywhere yet."

"My brother Eliezer's got a place he isn't using right now. Maybe he'd let you stay there. It needs a bit of work done to it, but that shouldn't trouble you as a carpenter."

"How did you know what my trade was?"

"Easy, love. Just take one look at your hands and there's a bag of tools down by that donkey. Anyways, I'll tell him to stop by."

I'd just got some water when he turned up, a small, middle aged man looking like he knew what he was about. His cloak must have cost a fortune and he had a gold chain round his neck, but he seemed friendly.

"Joe, is it? Eliezer's the name. Hear you've met my sister Hannah."

"Yes. She was marvelous yesterday when we had our son. We'd have been lost without her."

"She's never happier than when she's delivering a baby. But she tells me you've got nowhere to stay and his honor wants you out of here!" He grinned, bowing toward the inn.

"I'm afraid so. Our home's up north, and I'm not, we're just here to register."

"You're in for a long wait, I'm afraid. They've got themselves in a right muddle."

"I've seen some folk sleeping rough, I suppose they're waiting, and I guess we'll have to do the same."

"That's not a good idea with a new baby. But I might be able to help. I've got an old house that's standing empty."

"Eh ... Hannah did say something."

"Probably she told you the state it's in. But if you don't mind hard work, you're welcome to it."

I tried to remember what money we had left. "What rent are you asking?"

He smiled. "If you fixed the roof and cleaned it out, that would about cover things for now. Care to have a look?"

I had a shock when we got there. The door hung by one hinge, the dogs had made a frightful mess inside, and I could see the sky through a hole in the roof. But the walls felt solid enough; the rain hadn't got to them yet.

"Sorry, Joe, it's worse than I thought. I've not been here for a while. No hard feelings if you try elsewhere."

"Oh don't worry, I've handled worse than this. If it's all right by you, we'll move in. I just need some bricks, matting, and wood, and I'll fix it up in no time."

"Good. I'll show you my workshop; there's quite a bit of stuff there. My men will let you have what you want."

"But are you sure you want me to do this? You don't know the first thing about me."

"I've not been knocking around all these years without being able to size folk up. I reckon you'll do."

He returned at midday as I was smoothing off a new door post. He ran his hand along the wood. "Nothing wrong with that! You know what you're doing."

"I should do. Been at it all my life."

"Well, if the rest of your work is as good, I won't complain. See here, I don't know how long you reckon on staying, but I can always put some work your way."

"Are you looking for a carpenter?"

"I certainly am. My last one was a sight too keen on the wine skin!"

Then I looked at him carefully. "By the way, I hope you don't mind me asking, but what do you do?"

He laughed. "Plenty. For starters, I own most of Bethlehem and a few other villages around. That's a lot of property, and there are generally things that need doing. And if I run out of work, there's always Herod."

"He's still doing a lot of building, I hear."

"More than ever, and always looking out for craftsmen. Pays them well too, though I must say my men aren't sorry to come back to me!"

"Well, I spent a month working on one of his palaces in Damascus."

He nodded. "I've got a couple of warehouses up there."

"You have?"

"Yes, in fact, I've got them all over the place and caravans working most of the routes between. You're lucky to catch me; I just got back from Egypt. If you don't mind the journey, there's a lot going on in Alexandria."

Then he squinted at the sun. "Hey! Time I was off. But one thing I meant to ask, if you're registering here, you must have family around."

"My grandfather Matthan came from here."

"Matthan? Sounds familiar. Father had an uncle called that. Moved up north before I was born."

"Could be the same man. We may be related."

"My mother's still alive. I'll ask her; she knows all the family history."

I patched up the door. It still needed some more work, but it'd keep the dogs out. Then I got some matting from Eliezer's store to cover the hole in the roof. I'd just got back when I heard Mary outside. She was carrying Jesus strapped to her back.

"Come in and have a look," I said. "I'm sorry the floor's filthy. I'm just about to sweep it."

"It can't be worse than that stable!" she laughed. "This is fine; it's plenty big enough for the three of us."

She sat on a bench, but I knew she was itching to tell me some news. "Joe. Something lovely happened as I was coming here. There was this old lady—I'd never seen her before, but she must have known about Jesus."

"She did?"

"Yes, she came right up to me and had a good look at him. Then she asked if this was the new king. She was thrilled when I said he was."

"How did she know?"

"It must have been those shepherds. They've been telling everyone! It's the talk of the town."

"Did anyone else speak to you?"

"Oh yes, in no time there was a crowd round us wanting a look. That's why I've been so long."

We slept well in our new home. It was good to have somewhere where you didn't have to watch where you were treading. I woke up next morning staring at the hole in the ceiling.

"Are you going to fix that today?" Mary asked.

"Well, I've got the stuff for it, but I'm afraid it'll have to wait. I must get registered first."

"I'd forgotten about that. I won't be long, then I'll join you. I'll just get Jesus ready."

"I think I better go by myself. They say it takes hours, and I don't want you hanging around with the baby."

I'd hoped to get there early before too many people turned up, but I heard the din before I reached the street corner. The next road was jammed solid and all I could see were people's backs.

Suddenly, the crowd started heaving, and with a lot of shoving, a couple forced their way out, waving happily to friends nearby.

"Lucky them!" the man next to me remarked. "They must have got registered and be pushing off home. I only wish we could!"

"This crowd's awful," I replied. "I'm glad I stopped my wife coming."

"That's funny, I reckon most men bring their women along too, to fetch them wine and stuff while they're waiting."

"But mine had a baby two days ago. I don't want her standing around all day in the sun with the youngster."

"So why don't you come back in a day or two; then there won't be so many people. Anyway, they're stopping early today; Sabbath starts this evening."

"Suppose I better go then," I murmured, and I was just squeezing past him when he spoke again.

"You said your wife's just had a baby?"

"Yes, a son."

"He's not that king that everyone's talking about?"

I finally registered three days later. There were fewer folk by then, but it still took till midday before I was close enough to see what was going on.

There was a trestle table with three men sitting at it, writing on tablets. A soldier was leaning against the wall, and when the crowd got too close, he stirred himself and drove them back with the butt end of his spear.

Every time anyone finished, there was a mad scramble to take his place. I'd almost reached the table when the three scribes got up, stretched themselves, and tidied their tablets and pens away.

"Typical!" someone remarked. "Siesta! I doubt they'll be back inside three hours. We'll roast if we want to keep our place!" I stood there till late afternoon, and I never remember feeling so hot in my life. But at last it was my turn. Then the questions started. "Name ... Tribe ... Family ... Father's name ... Residence ..."

The list went on and on, and the scribes wrote down the replies very slowly, stopping every now and again to check something.

When I got back home Mary looked very relieved.

"Thank goodness that's done, Joe! I don't know how you could stand there all day in the sun! You must be gasping for something to drink."

"It won't come amiss!"

"And if we can tidy everything up tomorrow, we should be able to catch Isaac's party going home."

I shook my head. "No. I think we'd better miss it. We'd have to circumcise Jesus while we're traveling, and I doubt Isaac would be happy about that. And there's your purification too, better not travel while you're unclean,"

Mary nodded, "Well, he does make quite a fuss."

"I think it'd be much easier if we stayed here. We don't have to return for anything."

"But what about your mother?"

"She told me not to hurry back. We should be able to find another party going north later, and with luck, they'll be more cheerful than the last lot!"

She looked at me carefully. "Do you really want to go home?"

I sighed. "No. These last few months have been awful. It's such a joy to be away from all the gossip. I wish we could make a fresh start here."

CHAPTER ELEVEN

"Is your wife here?" A woman was standing in the doorway.

I found Mary outside. She'd just washed her robe and had put on my spare one. It hung round her in folds.

"A lady out there wants a word with you."

"Joe! I can't go like this!"

"Why not? I'm sure she's seen worse!"

Reluctantly, she followed me to the door where the woman was holding a robe. "Could you use this? It was my sister's; she died last Passover, and she looked about your size. She won't be needing it again!"

Mary burst into tears. "It's just what I wanted."

After that, quite a few folk turned up with gifts. Even Tom came one evening looking rather sheepish. "Hannah reckoned as you could use these. No hard feelings I'm sure!" And he gave us two cheeses.

His wife came in every day to check Mary and Jesus. One morning, she spoke to me.

"So are we ready to circumcise him?"

'Oh ... eh ... yes, of course."

She was counting on her fingers. "Let's see. He was born two days before Sabbath, so I reckon tomorrow will be the right time, the eighth day ..."

"But who'll do it for us?"

"Surely you know that? It's the father's job."

I swallowed nervously. "Yes, of course."

She looked at me carefully. "You'll want a knife."

"I've got one in my bag."

"Come on, Joe! You know better than that! It's got to be made of flint. The priests insist on using stone as they reckon metal's impure."

"I suppose I could borrow one from somewhere."

She laughed. "I thought you'd forget! Look here, I've got one for you. I know you'll be careful."

It was odd handling flint after using iron tools, but as I ran my thumb over the cutting edge, it felt sharp.

"Yes, this'll be all right."

"And so it should be! It's done all my boys!"

Then I remembered that at home a circumcision was an excuse for a party, but since we were strangers here, I didn't know who to invite. All the same, Mary insisted on sweeping the floor in case someone came.

Then Hannah appeared. "All right, are we? Want a hand getting things ready? Eliezer's found a load of your husband's relatives. They'll be along soon."

Mary looked alarmed. "How many are we expecting?"

"Enough to fill this place and then some."

"But ... we don't have enough wine; I'm sure our guests will want to drink his health."

Hannah laughed. "Yes, I thought of that. I've got a skin of Tom's best outside on a donkey. I'm sure he won't grudge you that if I talk to him nicely!"

And soon our room filled up with village folk together with two shepherds who slipped in at the back. Eliezer hurried by at the last moment, wiping his hands.

"Sorry I'm late, Joe. I had to check some stuff that's just come in from Damascus."

I was nervous about what I had to do since it was my first time, but it proved easy enough and the child didn't cry much. Afterward, we prayed over him, and I asked Eliezer to give the blessing. Then we named him Jesus just like Gabriel had said.

"Is that a family name?" Hannah asked.

"No, but we think it suits him."

She smiled. "I suppose an angel suggested that!"

"Yes, he did actually. I suppose you know it's another form of the name Joshua?"

She nodded and smiled down at him. "So little Joshua, are you going to be a fighter? One thing's for sure, you're the spitting image of your dad!"

We were just starting the festivities when Eliezer caught my eye. "I see you've got some of your shepherd friends here. I've heard the odd rumor or two, so I wonder if they'd mind telling us what really happened that night."

After a bit of a delay, the lad who'd come to us the next morning stepped forward. He was very shy and kept his eyes down as he explained how the angels had appeared to them.

But when he got to the bit about the new king, he walked over to Mary and looked down at Jesus.

"That's him right enough."

After our visitors had left, we talked. Mary was full of praise for the young shepherd.

"It took a lot of courage to speak like that in front of everyone."

"Yes, he was very good. But I was hoping to keep things quiet a bit longer."

"Are you scared about people knowing who Jesus is?"

"Well, think what'd happen if the story got out. That whole idea of him being a king won't go over well with Herod or the Romans either."

"It's too late now, Joe; the story's bound to spread. We'll just have to trust God to look after us."

We stood together watching him. Then she took my hand.

"Joe! He's smiling!"

"Maybe he's just got a bit of wind."

She didn't answer, but her face said it all.

I was very busy the next few weeks. After I'd finished the repairs on the house, Eliezer came around one morning sounding very pleased.

"That's fine work, Joe, and you've done it much quicker than I expected. I doubt it's ever looked so good. Now if you're interested, I've got a job down at the warehouse. It's rather tricky; one of the beams has gone rotten ..."

After that, I was working most hours and I didn't get as much time with Mary and Jesus as I'd have liked. I thought she was getting back to normal, but then I began to sense something was wrong.

Several times when I came in, I found her sitting and staring into the distance looking very depressed, and once she was crying. She tried to hide it when she saw me, but I knew she was unhappy, so I decided to speak to Hannah.

"Don't worry, Joe; it's quite normal. Most of my mothers get weepy when they've had a baby. It's funny: one moment they feel on top of the world, the next everything's black and they think they'll never cope!"

"So it's not my fault?"

She laughed. "Oh no, bless you, love! You've been a great support. But I expect she's missing her mum."

"So what should I do?"

"You've just got to love her! Put your arm round her! Tell her she's special. That sort of thing does a lot for a girl. And by the way, Eliezer thinks a lot of you too. I shouldn't be telling you this, but he reckons you're one of the best men he's got."

As usual, I was late back that evening and Mary had put Jesus down to sleep. After we'd eaten, we sat together in the lamplight.

"Mary, I've been thinking. Do you want to go back to Nazareth?"

"It's up to you. I know your work's going well, but I'm worried about your mother."

"Yes. We ought to find out how she is. And there's all your family too."

She smiled sadly. "I'm sure they'll be doing all right without me. But I suppose I ought to show them the baby."

"So when do you think we should go? Straight away?"

"I'm happy to start whenever you like. But I know your mother suggested that we wait till I'd had my purification. It would be nice to do that at the Temple now we're so close. Then we'll go home after that."

I remember hearing about this ceremony from Ezra years ago. He said women have to have a special cleansing after they'd had a baby. But I didn't take much notice at the time.

"So when do you have to have this?"

"Forty days from the day the boy was born; that'll be in a couple of weeks. But it would have been eighty days if I'd had a girl."

"Why's that?"

"I don't know, but it's in the law. You'd have to ask a Pharisee. They're a funny lot; they seem to spend all their time worrying if folk are unclean."

"And I seem to remember you have to make a sacrifice before you're cleansed?"

She nodded. "We can just give a couple of doves or pigeons as we're too poor to afford a lamb. We'll buy them when we get to the Temple. And we've also got to make an extra offering for Jesus because he's our firstborn."

"Redeeming him or something? I remember my brother Simon doing that for his eldest. Does that mean another sacrifice?"

"I'm afraid so."

"I hope it won't cost a lot! I've haven't earned much yet!"

"Don't worry, Joe! God'll find us what we need!"

Eliezer had been away on business, but I caught up with him one afternoon.

"I'm afraid I won't be in tomorrow. Mary's due for her purification and we're redeeming Jesus at the same time seeing as he's our firstborn."

"Is it that time already? It seems only yesterday you circumcised him! Suppose you'll be getting that done at the synagogue?"

"No, we're off to the Temple. It'd be a shame not to go since we've got the opportunity."

"Watch yourselves when you go there, and keep an eye on those priests. They'd cheat their own grandmothers given half a chance."

"Don't worry; I'll keep my wits about me!"

"I only hope you do! I think they're getting worse every year. And they've got the cheek to treat us traders as robbers! We're babes in arms compared with them!"

CHAPTER TWELVE

We started at first light, joining folk from the village who were taking produce to market in Jerusalem. There was even a shepherd with some of his flock.

Soon we reached the edge of the Hinnon Valley and our first view of Jerusalem. Mary lifted up the baby, "Look, Jesus! We're going to that lovely white Temple over there!"

I smiled. I didn't reckon he'd take much notice! But it was quite a sight: the city walls and Temple gleaming white in the morning sun while ahead of us was the aqueduct the Romans had built to supply the city's water.

But there were also smells. Much of the city's rubbish was burnt here, and since it was a windy day, smoke kept blowing in our faces. The shepherd too was having trouble leading his animals. "I fancy they be scared, as they know the gates of hell be here about," he explained.

"But surely that's just an old story?" I remarked.

"No, sir, I sees it myself with my own eyes. There was flames coming out of a hole in the ground and folks screaming ..."

Mary was frowning. "I don't know about hell, but they used to sacrifice babies here to the god Molech till King

Josiah put a stop to it!" Then she held Jesus tight. "No one's going to burn you, my love."

It was a sharp pull up the path to the Dung Gate. Here we left the others, promising to meet up again at the time of the evening sacrifice.

Mary was looking at the marble paving stones. "Pity we can't have a few of these in Nazareth!"

I smiled. "It would certainly brighten up the place!"

Then we passed the walls of a large house. Through the gateway, we could see a beautiful courtyard with palm trees and a fountain.

"How do you fancy living there, Joe?" She laughed.

"It's just my style. Perhaps we should put in an offer for it!"

We went through a market where the smell of spices took me right back to Sepphoris. When I went there as a lad, I used to imagine the wonderful meals we'd have if we could get hold of some of them!

Then we squeezed into a doorway as some of Herod's troops swaggered down the street. "I wouldn't care to argue with them!" I murmured to Mary.

After they'd passed, an old woman spat on the ground. "God curse them! The blasphemers!"

Finally we came to the Cheesemaker's Valley, a deep gorge with the city on one side and the Temple mount on the other. And although I had seen it so often, I still gasped at the walls looming up ahead with marble so white that it hurt my eyes.

Mary stared. "I've never seen it look better!"

"You should come here at dawn. The stone's deep pink then, turning gold as the sun comes up. I reckon it beats all the gilding on the Temple!"

We crossed the valley using the Royal Bridge, a magnificent structure so wide you could have marched a legion across twenty men abreast. When we got to the middle, Mary leaned over the parapet.

"Look, Jesus! Those toys down there, they're real houses!" Then she turned, "And do you see those hills? There's Bethlehem, where you were born!"

I was peering at the bridge itself. It was made of huge stones, and I couldn't imagine how they ever got them up here, let alone fit them together with joints I'd have been proud of.

We entered the Temple enclosure through a triple arch. I gazed at the marble columns, which seemed to go up and up into the sky. On previous visits, I'd been part of a group from Nazareth out to enjoy ourselves, but now with just the three of us, I had time to look round and I felt utterly insignificant, a mere ant crawling over the ground.

But there was no time to brood; we were out in the open again in the Court of the Gentiles. This was a huge square, each side three hundred paces long and surrounded by colonnades ten times the height of a man, one of the wonders of the world.

Everyone was allowed in this outer court, and it was crowded. "Wait here long enough," my father used to say, "and you'll see every man on the face of the earth!"

There were the usual Greeks and Romans milling around, Ethiopians and Indians with their strange robes, and even fair-haired men with blue eyes wearing trousers and cloaks fastened with gold clasps.

"They're Celts from the far north," I explained to Mary. "I saw some once in Damascus. They say they live in forests."

We pushed through the crowds toward the Temple buildings. "This is what I hate," I grumbled, "changing our money for that wretched Temple currency."

"But what's wrong with our coins?" Mary asked.

"They've got Caesar's head on them, and the priests say that makes them blasphemous. But it doesn't stop them spending them once they're outside!"

There was a row of tables. During a feast, you could wait hours to get served, but today there were only a few people ahead of us, and I just had time to compare the different rates. But the Temple would make a profit whichever one we chose.

"Next!" The man at the table pulled my pile of money toward him, checking it through. "This one's no good!" he grunted, throwing the coin back across the table. Then he made a mark on a wax tablet and pushed some Temple currency over. I picked it up, but there were very few coins considering what I'd given him.

"I know I didn't have much money to change," I sighed as we walked away, "but it was all I had and I worked hard for it. That bloke couldn't even be bothered to lift his head to look at me!"

Mary squeezed my hand. "Never mind! I like looking at you! Come on, the baths are over there. It's time to get cleansed."

I know God wanted us to be pure when we went into the Temple, but this ritual washing seemed a waste of time. You went down steps into a pool, the mikveh, and put your head right under before you could climb up the other side. I hated to think who had been in there before me!

Father cleaned one out once. It took a morning to drain the stale water; then a day to dig out the thick layer of sludge from the bottom. "If you've got to go in one of those things, Joe, make sure it's just rained and the water's fresh!"

As Mary was going toward the women's side, I remembered the baby.

"Want me to have Jesus while you go in?"

She shook her head. "No, I'll take him. I'm sure one of the women will hold him while I go down, then I can dip him afterwards."

I didn't like wandering around in wet clothes waiting for the sun to dry me, and I hated the smell. When Mary joined me again, I muttered, "Wish I could have a bath to wash this holy water off!"

She smiled. "Elizabeth was saying that some rich people do just that. But the Pharisees argue it makes you unclean again!"

Now we had to buy our sacrifice. There was a regular market ahead and the din was terrific with cattle lowing and sheep bleating. "I feel sorry for the animals," I shouted to Mary. "They must know what's going to happen!"

She nodded sadly. We passed a stall with cattle. Two or three well-dressed men were walking round prodding them carefully. They looked for all the world like rich farmers choosing their herd.

The sheep were just beyond. Less well-off worshippers bought these, though they were still well beyond my means. Instead, we headed toward the birds.

There were huge cages filled with sad looking pigeons and doves. We had a long wait till it was our turn.

"So what do you want?" the man asked.

"An offering for my wife's cleansing after childbirth and for our new son seeing as he's our first born."

"You'll need two birds," he replied and, without waiting for a reply, reached in and felt round until he had caught a couple. As I stepped forward to take them, he released them into another cage.

"But aren't we supposed to give them to the priest for sacrifice?"

"It's too much trouble. He waits to the end of the day then does them all together. Stick your money in that box over there."

I turned to Mary. "I thought we'd have some part in this."

"Never mind, Joe. God knows we've done our best, and he's pleased with us."

After paying, we walked on round to the east side of the Temple and the steps leading to the next court. Gentiles weren't allowed any further, and there was a big sign warning them they'd be killed if they tried.

This section was known as the Court of the Women because that's as far as they were allowed to go. Some were praying by the far wall, but mostly we saw priests hurrying in and out of a large doorway.

High above us was the great east wall of the Temple glistening with marble and gold. But stuck right in the middle was a large gilded eagle.

"What's that doing there?" Mary asked. She sounded shocked.

"I heard Herod had put it up there to keep his Roman friends happy."

"But the priests won't like it."

"They're livid; they've kept telling him it's a blasphemy, breaking the commandment that says you mustn't make images of animals. But he won't listen. It wouldn't be so bad if he'd stuck it round a corner, but you can't miss it up there."

"And I suppose that's the Treasury through that door?"

I nodded. "Yes, and see the trumpets over there? When I was a lad, I hoped the priests would blow them, but they're really collection boxes. You put your money in the narrow bit on top and it falls into the wider part that looks like a bell."

Then Mary spoke. "I've got to find out which one to put my offering in."

The priest was standing on the steps looking very bored with a string of women waiting to speak to him.

When it came to Mary's turn, he wiped his nose on his sleeve before half bending his head toward her.

"Excuse me, sir, but I've got to make an offering for my baby seeing as he's our first born."

"Five shekels. End trumpet."

She looked embarrassed. "I'm very sorry, sir, but we don't have five shekels. I've only got four."

He shrugged. "Four shekels then. Put them in the box!"

Some women waiting behind tittered, and she went bright red. By the time she'd made her offering, she was crying.

"The Temple's not our place," I said gently.

"No. I suppose I'm being silly, but I thought today would be special, what with those shepherds coming to see our baby and the folk being excited about him. But here we're being treated like we're nothing."

"It's the priests that really get me," I complained, "lifting their noses like we hadn't washed!"

"And I know this place is really lovely and holy, but I feel so small somehow!"

I put my arm round her. "I'm just the same. But never mind, next time we come we'll have some friends with us. And we'll feel better once we get home."

It was then that I saw him, an old man hobbling along as fast as possible. He stopped right in front of us and stared at Jesus with an ecstatic expression on his face.

CHAPTER THIRTEEN

Suddenly, to our astonishment, he threw his arms in the air and began praising God. To start with, his voice was shaky but it soon strengthened.

Then he reached out his arms and Mary gave him Jesus to hold.

"Mary!" I whispered. "Is he safe? He looks very frail."

As she turned round, I saw she had a faraway look. "Oh yes, Joe, he's safe. You can tell that man's used to handling babies by the way he's holding him."

The man had started praying and the odd thing was he sounded just like the shepherds. He was talking to God like he really knew him. Then I realized he was making up a new psalm, just as Mary had.

"Lord, you've kept your promise,
So now you can let your servant go in peace.
With my own eyes I've seen your salvation
Which you've prepared for everyone to see,
A light which will bring revelation to the Gentiles
And be the glory of your people Israel."

My mouth dropped open. I couldn't believe what I was hearing and here of all places, in this huge Temple with its large crowds. But this was a stranger who knew just who Jesus was, and it wasn't as if there was anything special about us to make us stand out, just an ordinary couple with a baby. But somehow, he'd found us.

Then from the corner of my eye, I saw Mary had raised her arms too and was praising God. And suddenly I felt very humble.

After he'd finished praying, he stood gazing at the baby, then he raised his head. His eyes were really piercing; I think the old prophets must have looked like that.

Very carefully, he passed Jesus back to Mary, then spoke to both of us. "Forgive me, my children. I have been remiss. I should have introduced myself. My name is Simeon."

"I'm Joseph, this is my wife Mary, and we've called our son Jesus."

"Well, many years ago the Holy Spirit of God gave me a very special promise. He said I would not die until I had seen the Lord's anointed one, his Messiah. It has been a long time, but today I felt God telling me to come to the Temple. And he showed me the very one whom I have been waiting for!"

Then he looked straight at me. "And I know he has spoken to you too. If you permit me, I would like to bless you both because you have been given a very special task, looking after this precious one."

He put his hands on our heads; they felt surprisingly firm. Then very simply he asked God's blessing and protection on us.

Afterward, he turned to Mary. I could see him gazing at her as if willing her to understand what he would say.

"Your son has a very special destiny, but it will not be easy

And many will wish him harm.

He will cause the ruin of many people in Israel and they will hate him,

But he will also lift many up.

Like the prophets of old he will be a sign

That will cause bitter argument,

And he will publicly show the innermost thoughts of many people."

He stopped. For a moment, I thought he'd finished, then I saw sweat on his brow. Something was troubling him, and he seemed to be groping for words.

Then he spoke very quietly to Mary, and I could only just hear what he said. "My daughter, a sword is going to piece your own heart."

It was hot in the court, but I felt as if a cloud had gone over the sun and I shivered. I knew then that something serious would happen.

I suppose I could have asked Simeon what this all meant, but it didn't seem the right time somehow. So I mumbled my thanks, and Mary smiled at him.

Then as we reached the stairway leading back to the Court of the Gentiles, I noticed an old woman coming toward us. She wore a shabby widow's gown and was bent right over. We paused to let her pass.

Suddenly she straightened up, and I noticed a look of awe in her eyes as she spotted the baby. Then she too began praising God for what he'd done and for letting her see Messiah.

I was amazed all over again. As far as I could tell, she'd been nowhere near us while Simeon was speaking, so it could only be God who had pointed Jesus out to her!

"Would you like to hold him?" Mary asked.

She reached out, then stood cuddling him. She was the happiest person I've ever seen.

"It's marvelous, just marvelous. The best moment of my life and I've enjoyed eighty-four summers. It's even better than the seven years I had with my husband!"

Another old woman had followed her. "Whose baby have you got there, Anna?"

"You may well ask! Look at him! This is the child God's sent to save Jerusalem! He's the Messiah we've been waiting for!"

She was so excited that she showed him to everybody. And he seemed quite happy, not crying but just looking round solemnly.

I turned to an old man standing next to us. "Excuse me, sir, but do you know who she is?"

He laughed. "Everyone knows her, Old Anna, Phanuel's daughter. She must be one of the last people who can trace their family back to the tribe of Asher. She lives here."

"What? In the Temple?"

"That's right. Quite a few folks do. They spend all their time worshipping, praying, and fasting. You see, they're looking for Messiah and they reckon he'll come here first."

I glanced back at her, the picture of happiness, rocking the one she'd waited for all her life. We'd got quite a crowd round us by now, but then I saw a priest pushing his way up the steps.

"Come on! Get a move on! You can't stop here! You're blocking the way. People need to get through to worship."

As we walked back across the Court of the Gentiles, I looked at the various foreigners again. I was thinking how Simeon had told us that Jesus would be a light to them too. It was a pity that none of them had recognized him!

We were nearly at the bridge when we heard rams' horns blasting away behind us. I turned quickly to make sure Mary was keeping up.

"That's the evening sacrifice starting! We'll have to dash if we want to catch the others!"

Later, while we were walking home, Mary repeated everything Simeon and Anna had said. I was amazed. "I don't know how you can remember all that!"

"I think it's very important, something God's saying to us like those prophesies in the Scriptures."

I nodded. "Yes, and what a day we've had! I'd never have believed it. It wasn't even just Simeon but Anna as well. You know, until they turned up, I was beginning to wonder if God had forgotten us!"

"I wasn't feeling too happy either, Joe. Isn't it lovely how God keeps sending us folk to encourage us! And warn us too, don't forget. You know, it reminds me of a court of law."

"A court of law? What's that got to do with it?"

"Well, when you bring a case, you need at least two witnesses. We've just had our two, Simeon and Anna! They should remind us who Jesus is!"

We got home just before dark. And since Mary was no longer unclean, we could start our married life properly. It had been a long wait.

CHAPTER FOURTEEN

I enjoyed being in Bethlehem, what with having a pretty wife, a young son, and as much work as I wanted. And we'd got away from that awful gossip. But we had agreed that we should go home as soon as Mary was purified.

And I was also worried about Mother. She wasn't that old, but in the last year or so, she'd begun to look frail and I had a hunch we should go and see her soon.

I mentioned this to Mary the day after her purification.

"Yes, Joe, I think it would be a good idea. I'm sure your mother would love to see Jesus. And I'd also like to show him to my parents and friends."

"I'm not sure they'd be very pleased, judging by the way they treated you last time. And I don't know how we'll get back; Isaac and his friends left weeks ago."

"Couldn't you ask Eliezer? He's always got caravans going up that way."

"It's not as easy as that. I don't think he was happy about me taking yesterday off, so how will he feel about us going up north for a few weeks? He'll probably think we're going to stay there."

"Well, it is our home. Anyway, I thought you'd almost finished his work."

"He's got a lot more. For a start, he wants to rebuild his warehouse; it's not every day you get offered a job like that."

"But like you said, tell him you want to see your mother. We can always come back afterward. We might even bring her with us."

"I doubt she'd come; she's got all the family up there and her friends."

I didn't look forward to tackling Eliezer; he was by far and away the best boss I'd had and I didn't like messing him around. But next day as we were clearing the old warehouse, he bustled in and we started chatting. Then he looked hard at me.

"Joe! You seem worried. Tell me about it."

"Well … I've been thinking Mary and I ought to go back to Nazareth for a while …"

His face dropped. "To Nazareth? What now?"

"Yes. You see, there's my mother. She's not been well."

"So you want to see how she is?"

"Yes. I'm quite worried about her. And there are some other things that need sorting out. And Mary wants to show everyone the baby."

He smiled. "I expect there are a lot of folk looking forward to that! I won't put pressure on you, but I need to get on with this job and I'd like you to do it. With all those new contacts in Syria, we've got more stuff here than I've got space for."

"I know."

"So how long will you be? Two weeks? I might be able to hold the job that long."

"That should be fine. But we've still got to find a group going north and that might take time."

"I've got some men leaving for Syria tomorrow. You're welcome to join them."

I tried to hide my relief. "Oh thank you ..."

"And I can lend you a mule to carry things."

"Thanks. But we've got a donkey."

"I know! I've never seen such a bag of bones! I doubt if it'd make Jerusalem, let alone Galilee. You better borrow one of mine."

We left at dawn with three of Eliezer's men. Mary was walking this time with Jesus strapped to her back while I guided the mule.

Our first stop was Jerusalem to meet the main caravan. I thought we might be waiting all morning, but they were already loaded up ready to go.

"No time for dawdling!" the leader called. "Or we'll have Eliezer on our tail!"

"But which way are we going?" I asked as we headed past the Roman fortress of Antonia.

"Out through the Fish Gate."

"Isn't that the wrong way for Jericho?"

"We're going through Samaria; it's much quicker."

"But isn't it dangerous?"

"There's nothing wrong with them Samaritans if you treat 'em right. I reckon you've been listening to too many rabbis!"

"Aren't you afraid of being robbed?"

He pulled a knife out of his belt. "I think we can look after ourselves! We've been on that road a few times!"

By noon on the second day we'd got to Sychar.

"I've always wanted to come here," Mary remarked. "It was one of the first plots of land the Israelites owned. Jacob bought it and later they buried Joseph here."

"I must say the well's very welcome on a hot day!" I said. "I could do with a cup of cold water."

We reached Sebaste that evening. It was King Ahab's old capital: he might have been evil, but he knew how to pick a good spot! It's on top of a hill and you can see for miles over the plain of Jezreel. It's very much a pagan city: high walls, a forum, and a long street with colonnades and masses of shops. And everywhere you can see round towers and pagan temples.

But to my surprise, Mary was quite interested. "What's that place over there, Joe?"

"That temple? I think it's where they worship the emperor."

She shuddered. "So is it right that Herod built it?"

"Yes, it was a thank you to his Roman master. If it wasn't for Augustus, he wouldn't be king now."

"But how could he build a pagan temple and the one in Jerusalem at the same time?"

"I don't know! Maybe he was wondering which god was going to win!"

We reached Nazareth the next afternoon. The mule team stopped at the foot of the hill and the leader explained, "If you want to come back with us, we'll be stopping in Sepphoris in ten days' time."

We toiled upward in the heat. It seemed to take even longer than ever, and now I was so close to home I was really worrying.

At last we reached a bend in the path from where we could see our house. I also spotted Simon and waved to him. As soon as he noticed us, he started heading in our direction, and when he got close, I could see that he was worried.

"How's Mother?" I asked as we began walking back up the hill.

"She's waiting for you in her house," he said quietly.

"Is she all right?"

He hesitated. "Joe. I'm sorry, but she's not too well. I think you better come with me right away."

"I'll look after things here while you go in," Mary insisted.

Mother was lying on a pallet with a lamp beside her. For a moment, I thought she was asleep; then Miriam, who had been bending over her, spoke.

"Joseph's here, Mother."

I knelt and took her hand. "It's me. Joe!"

I started wiping her forehead, then her eyes flickered and she tried to say something.

"I'm sorry Joe," Miriam said, "but we couldn't warn you. We didn't know when you were coming back."

"How long has she been like this?"

"She was fine till yesterday. But in the morning when I came in, she was lying on the floor. I called Simon and we tried to get her up, but she couldn't stand."

Simon broke in. "We put her on her pallet and gave her some wine with myrrh in it. And we made sure there was someone with her."

"It's good you were on hand."

"It's Miriam you need to thank. She's been here most of the time."

"Has Mother eaten anything?"

"No. We got a bit of milk down her, but she won't touch anything else."

Just then she opened her eyes. "Joseph, is that you?"

"Yes, Mother. We're come home."

She clasped my hand. Then she started muttering something and I caught the word "baby."

I hurried out and called Mary. She brought Jesus in and, bending down, put him in Mother's arms, watching to see that he didn't slip out.

"Here he is! You've got him."

Mother opened her eyes again. She moved her hand to stroke his head. Then she smiled.

Jesus had woken up and wriggled a bit, but fortunately he didn't cry. They lay there together for a little, then she started groaning and Mary picked him up.

"Joe, I'll take him outside for the moment. Ask Simon if he's got any more of that myrrh to give her."

I sat with her for a long time. Then Mary came back with a second lamp. The flame flickered up for a moment, and I saw her face was wet.

"Oh Joe! I'm so sorry!"

"It's the end, isn't it?"

"Yes. I think so." Then she burst into tears. "She was like a mother to me. I'll miss her much more than I will my own!"

Mother died in the night, and next day we buried her beside my father. It didn't take long to sort her things out, and I was shocked to find how little food she had in the house.

Then Miriam cornered me. "So what do you propose doing now?"

"I really don't know. Maybe we'll go back to Bethlehem for a bit. I've got a lot of work there."

She laughed. "I might have guessed. It took you long enough to come back! And you left me to cope with Mother! It's not your fault she wasn't dead and buried before you honored us with your presence!"

"That's not fair! I spent years looking after her! How was I to know she'd fall ill when I was away? Anyway, she told us not to hurry back in case we had any problems with the baby."

She snorted. "Baby! That's all you care about! Don't you know you've brought shame on the whole family? I can hardly hold my head up when I meet my friends!"

"I was hoping that business would have blown over by now."

"Blow over when you have the neck to bring your brat here and parade it in front of everyone! I doubt there's anyone in Nazareth who'd pass the time of day with you two now!"

And so it proved. Mary went along to see her parents, but she didn't stay long. When she came back, she looked close to tears.

"How did you get on?"

"I suppose it could have been worse. They did ask me in."

"And what did they think of Jesus?"

"They hardly looked at him. He might as well have been any other village kid."

And in the next few days, she became more and more discouraged. One so-called friend after another ignored or insulted her. Once more, she was reduced to collecting water from the well at noon when no one else was around, and some of the children even started throwing stones at her. There seemed no chance we could ever live back in Nazareth.

One evening, I turned to her. "So what do you think we should do now?"

She sighed. "Well, rightly speaking, this is our home. But I suppose we'd be better off in Bethlehem if Eliezer's still got that work for you."

"But this seems so unfair. If only we could explain what had really happened to us."

"Life is unfair, Joe; I suppose that's why Simeon warned me that things would be difficult. I don't mind so much for myself, but isn't it awful how everyone treats our beautiful baby like a bit of rubbish?"

I had a word with Simon next day. He agreed to keep an eye on our house while we were away, although I suspected he hoped we wouldn't be back too soon.

Then it was time to go over to Sepphoris to meet Eliezer's caravan. As we climbed out of Nazareth for the last time, I looked back and wondered if I'd ever see my home again.

CHAPTER FIFTEEN

Eliezer met us in Jerusalem when the caravan got in. He was so busy checking everything that it was some time before he turned to me.

"So you didn't stay long then?"

"No. My mother died just after we got there, and there didn't seem any point in hanging around."

He put his hand on my shoulder. "I'm sorry, Joe. Get yourself sorted out, and I'll come round and see you. The house is all ready for you."

He dropped in two evenings later.

"I don't want to rush you, but there is a lot to do on that warehouse. The other man I hired doesn't know one end of a saw from the other!"

I grinned. "I'll be right along!"

It was hard work, and for the next two months, I was busy all the hours of daylight, but at least it kept me from grieving too much for Mother. Eliezer had found me a good team of laborers, and they did everything the way I liked.

We were tidying up one day when he appeared, slapping the doorpost as he walked in. "My! That feels solid! It should stand up for a few years!"

"Well, I always try to give satisfaction!"

"It looks like it too, and you haven't wasted any time! That other lazy so-and-so reckoned it would take six months or more!"

"Bah! You Southerners don't know what work is! They don't pay us to sit around in Nazareth!"

He laughed. "You slave driver! Well, you'll be glad to know there are a few more jobs like that! Trouble is, though, I've got to leave you just now. I've got a little problem down in Egypt."

"Nothing too serious, I hope?"

"It sounds like some of my staff have been helping themselves to the stock. Only heard last night, but I've got to go and sort them out."

"What shall I do while you're away?"

"A bit of maintenance, perhaps; there are always things that need fixing."

"I'll have a look around."

"But don't let me stand in your way if somebody offers you a job while I'm gone. Only I'd like to see you back here in a month."

The break gave us a chance to visit Elizabeth and Zechariah. They didn't live far from Bethlehem, and we got there in a morning.

It was almost like Elizabeth was waiting for us. As we arrived, she came straight out and threw her arms round Mary. Then she called Zechariah and he came out too. There didn't seem anything wrong with his speech despite what we'd heard.

They were thrilled to see Jesus. Elizabeth held him for a while, then passed him to her husband, who prayed a blessing over him. I felt a lump in my throat as I realized how often he must have recited those ancient words without ever thinking that one day he'd do it over Messiah.

Then they invited us in. A baby was crawling on the floor, and Elizabeth picked him up and turned to Mary. "Here's our John! Our special one."

"He's lovely. I've been longing to see him. But how did you manage with the birth?"

"The Lord was good to me; it was very easy, though I must admit I was dreading it. Thank you for all your prayers."

"Everybody must have been excited!"

"You've never seen anything like it. I reckon the whole village came round to see him, and they were all praising God."

I turned to Zechariah. "And sir, it must have been a great joy for you to circumcise him."

He sighed. "No! I did not have that pleasure. You see, I still had my affliction. You must ask Elizabeth about that."

She smiled. "One of my brothers took charge, and it went all right till it came to the naming. He was all for calling him Zechariah after his father, but I told him the name was John. I had to be quite firm with him."

Mary looked surprised. "How awkward!"

"Yes, the men were quite upset and told me it wasn't a family name. But then someone thought of checking with my husband. They wrote on his wax tablet asking what name he wanted, and he replied, 'His name is John!' in huge letters."

"So that settled it?"

Elizabeth chuckled. "It certainly did! And at that moment, my husband got his voice back. I've never heard anyone praise God like that! He must have been saving up the whole nine months!"

Mary looked wistful. "I wish I'd been there!"

"You'd have loved it. Everybody was so excited. I reckon the whole of Judea's heard about John by now. And you know people are still coming to see him."

Zechariah broke in then. "And I have also been able to tell people what Gabriel said to me! Our John is to be set aside for God and he must never drink wine. Also I was told he would have the Spirit of God in him from the day he was born."

"Will he be a priest like you?" I asked.

"No, but he will bring his people back to God. He will have Elijah's spirit in him so he can unite families and punish the disobedient. And he will prepare the way for Messiah."

Then Elizabeth turned to him. "Perhaps, dear, you might like to sing them your psalm. The one you gave us that day.'

'What!' I exclaimed. "You've composed one too?'

"Yes, it came to me in those months when I couldn't speak, and it was a wonderful release when I was able to proclaim it aloud."

He leaned over and took John in his arms before he began.

"Praise the Lord, the God of Israel,

Because he has come and set his people free,

Setting his salvation in the house of his servant David

As his holy prophets promised long ago.

He has delivered us from our enemies and every hateful hand.

He has shown mercy to our ancestors as he solemnly promised Abraham

He has rescued us from our enemies so that all our lives

We can serve him freely having been made holy and righteous.

And you my child will be called a prophet of the Most High God

Who will go before the Master to prepare the way for him,

To tell the people they will be saved through the forgiveness of their sins.

Our God is tender and merciful; his salvation will come like sunrise

On those living in darkness under the shadow of death,

Guiding our feet into the path of peace."

When we got back to Bethlehem, Mary got a job working on the barley harvest. One evening, I remember her coming in hot and tired and pushing the hair back off her forehead.

"I reckon I know how Ruth felt!"

"Who?"

She laughed. "You must know! You're always on about your ancestor David! She was his great-grandmother, remember? And she worked on the barley harvest here in Bethlehem in these same fields all those years ago."

I grinned. "Oh yes, of course. Mother used to talk about her."

"But she had a much harder time than me. Fancy being a foreigner and a widow at that! But she did what she could and God blessed her. I reckon I could do a lot worse than copy her!"

I worked a couple of days in the fields too. It was good having Mary around. I kept catching sight of her and thinking how lovely she looked with Jesus in a sling on her back.

Saul was working there too. He was a man I'd got to know while we were building Eliezer's warehouse. One day, we were chatting when he said, "Joe, you're wasting your time here; a craftsman like you shouldn't be cutting barley! Why don't you try your luck over at Herodium?"

"What? You mean Herod's palace?"

"Yes, they're crying out for men there."

"But would they offer me anything? I only want a few weeks' work, till Eliezer gets back."

"It's worth a try; in fact, I fancy going there myself. But you've got to watch out for Herod—he's always coming up from Jericho. And they say his temper's got a lot worse recently. I wouldn't give much for your chances if you cross him."

I grunted. "From what I hear, nobody's safe. They reckoned he was crazy about his wife Mariamme, but he still killed her."

"And he strangled her sons Alexander and Aristobulus too. They were set up by their half-brother Antipater, who sold Herod a pack of lies."

"But hasn't that son gone off to Rome?"

"That's right! I guess he found the place too hot for him! Everybody's trying to stop him becoming king once his father dies!"

We went over to Herodium two days later. It's only five miles away, built on a flat-topped hill. It doesn't look too much from a distance, but close up, it's massive.

"So why did Herod choose this site?" I asked Saul. "It's in the middle of a desert!"

"It's a special place for him. His mother survived a nasty accident here and he won a victory locally, so he swore this is where he wanted to be buried. You can see his mausoleum there on the side of the hill waiting for him."

"It looks impressive."

"Wait till you get on top! He's even built a theatre, and as if the hill wasn't high enough already, he piled another huge mound of earth on top."

I didn't have any difficulty getting taken on, and in no time, I was on my way to a workshop. The palace was vast, room after room, done out in the latest fashion. I didn't look at the walls too much; they were covered in paintings of pagan gods showing off their private parts. But the furniture was wonderful.

One of the men was working on a table. I ran my hand down one leg.

"That's good work!"

He looked up and smiled. "We try our best! It wouldn't do to upset the boss!"

But it was not only the workmanship; I'd rarely seen anything like the wood he was using. They said it came from Africa, really heavy and black as night. It would take me years to earn enough to buy one plank!

It was a good time since I'd worked on quality wood, but it soon came back to me. The foreman picked up a joint I'd made and took it over to the light for a look, but he seemed happy enough.

A week later, Herod appeared. They'd brought him up from Jericho, where he spent most of his time wallowing in the hot springs.

"They say you have to watch yourself while he's around," Saul murmured. "You never know what sort of mood he's in."

The foreman nodded. "That's right sure enough! Last month he took a dislike to one of the Nubians. He signaled to the guards, and they dragged him off."

"What had he done?"

He shrugged. "Don't ask me. Nothing, most like. But they say Herod can read a man's thoughts. He'll stare into a newcomer's eyes, and if he's not happy, well ..."

"So what did they do to him?"

"Crucified him, more than likely; I didn't like to ask. His screams were bad enough."

Not much work was done that morning; we were busy sprucing the place up. Herod arrived just before midday carried in a litter by a team of sweating slaves. He looked to be around seventy and huge with it. I'd heard he was covered in sores, and he certainly swore as they lifted him onto a couch.

I was only a few paces away and could hear the rasping as he breathed. But what I remember most were his eyes peering out under hooded lids, cold as ice, moving all the time, looking for anyone who might stick a knife in his guts.

I shrank back, but then suddenly I noticed him looking directly at me. I tried to avoid his gaze, but he caught my eyes. I knew how a rat must feel just before a snake swallows it!

It felt like he was staring at me for hours, but it could only have been a few moments. Then he grunted and turned away to talk to somebody on the other side of the room. I spent the rest of the day in a cold sweat, waiting for a hand to grab me.

The foreman grinned when I came for my wages. "His Majesty seemed to take a fancy to you! Here's your money. See you tomorrow?"

I murmured something and he laughed. He knew I wouldn't be coming back. You couldn't have dragged me there for all the gold in the Temple!

CHAPTER SIXTEEN

If it hadn't been for the Magi, I reckon we'd still be in Bethlehem.

The first I heard was when Eliezer dropped by one afternoon. "You should have been up in town today, Joe! A bunch of Arab astrologers turned up from somewhere out east, Magi I think they're called."

"Oh yes. I remember seeing some in Sepphoris years ago."

"I doubt you saw any like these! They must have been princes at the very least with a huge caravan, camels, slaves, the lot. The money those folks must have—it'd make Croesus sit up and take notice!"

"Were they on their way to Rome?"

"No, funnily enough. It seems they'd come all this way just to visit Jerusalem. There was a rumor they were searching for a new king born round here."

"A new king? Herod isn't expecting any more sons, is he? I thought he was too busy getting rid of the ones he's got!"

"To be honest, I don't know; I just got the story off a client. One of those Magi fellows had been asking passersby where the king was and giving away gold pieces when he got an answer. He had half the city round him hoping for a handout!"

"Well, I'd like to know what Herod makes of it!"

"Plenty, I expect. He must have got wind of them because he arrived in town just as I was leaving. I expect he'll be having them in for questioning!"

We chatted on for a bit, then just as he was leaving, he looked at me.

"Joe, I've just had a thought about that king the Magi were on about. Wasn't that what those shepherds called your lad when he was born?"

That bought me up with a start. "Yes, that's right, they did. But I doubt these Magi, whoever they are, will want anything to do with us. They'll be looking for someone rich and important."

That evening, I couldn't get the thought of the shepherds' visit out of my head. To be honest, I'd almost forgotten about it till now, and as for Jesus, I'm afraid I was tending to think of him just as an ordinary toddler.

He was nearly two and growing fast. But he was very easy going; he never had temper tantrums or screamed if another child stole his toy.

We had to keep an eye on him, mind; he was into everything as soon as he could crawl. I don't think he was being naughty; he was just very bright and wanted to investigate everything. But if I once told him not to do something, he never tried it again.

What he liked best, though, was listening to Mary. Of course, being her first child, she had time to spend with him, and she told him all the usual children's stories. But his favorites came from the Scriptures.

He'd sit on her knee for hours, looking up at her and listening. And when he started talking, one of his first words was "Hallelujah," except that it came out as "Allujah!"

That really tickled the local rabbi, and he reminded me of it every time we met. He'd been rather wary of us after that business of the shepherds, but then one day, he heard Mary singing a psalm to Jesus in Hebrew. He couldn't get over how much of the Scriptures she knew, and after that, we were good friends. Sometimes he even let her read the sacred scrolls.

And he really took to Jesus. He was forever sitting him on his knee and telling him stories. He even wrote the Hebrew alphabet out on a piece of wood with a burnt stick. And pretty soon, the child had learned all the letters.

But I'm forgetting about the Magi. It was two days later; Mary had settled Jesus for the night and we were just lying down when we heard a noise outside. Then there was a banging on the door.

"Anyone at home?" someone was shouting in Greek.

I'd left a peep hole so I could take a squint at any visitor. I could see a man in a very strange robe, but he didn't look like anyone I knew and I wondered if I should keep quiet. But then something made me open the door.

The noise outside was terrific, and despite the dark, I could see quite well as there were men carrying torches. But it took me a while to make sense of it all.

There was a whole caravan out there. By our door were men in Arab clothes, and behind was a mass of camels and mules and slaves milling round. And further back still I could see our neighbors craning their necks to get a good view.

"Sir, I believe you have a young king living here." It was the man who had been knocking. His accent was so strange that it took me a moment to make out what he was saying.

"Eh ... I ..." I began, but then Mary tugged at my sleeve. "Joe. They've come to see Jesus!"

Then I remembered what Eliezer had been talking about. "Are you the men who were in Jerusalem the other day looking for a king?"

"Yes! The Most High God has directed us here. May I ask if we could have the honor of seeing him?"

"Well ... The trouble is we've only got one small room. But you are welcome to come into our humble home."

He spread his hands. "Do not concern yourselves. It would be a great honor if you would invite us in to see your special baby."

I glanced at Mary and she was nodding. "That's fine. Only please give me a moment while we rouse him."

It was a tight squeeze getting them in, although the servants stayed outside. Mary lit two lamps, then sat in a corner cradling Jesus. Having just woken up, he was rubbing his eyes.

Now that I could see the men properly, it was obvious they were very rich. Their robes must have cost a ransom, they all wore heavy gold jewelry, and they filled the room with the scent of exotic ointments.

The man who'd spoken to me knelt down and recited something in a strange language. I think it was a prayer because then he bowed over till his forehead touched the floor. In a moment, the others had knelt in front of Jesus too.

It was like the shepherds all over again. This time, of course, the floor was clean unlike that filthy cow shed and our visitors were dressed like royalty. But they seemed to have the same sense of awe as they worshipped.

I found a spot behind them and lay down myself, once again thanking God for his encouragement and the gift of this child. Then, suddenly, they all got up and lifted their arms high in the air. They were glowing with joy.

Jesus was wide awake now and smiling broadly. He wasn't frightened by these strange men; it was almost as if he'd been expecting them.

Then the first man turned to me. "Please excuse me, sir, for a moment."

He went outside and returned, followed by some servants carrying three polished wooden boxes.

"Sir, we would consider it an honor if we could give these small unworthy gifts to the king."

I didn't know what to say. "Yes ... eh ... thank you ..."

He knelt down in front of Jesus and, after bowing, offered Mary a box.

"It's heavy!" she exclaimed as she almost dropped it. The lid was held down by a catch, and as she tried to open it, Jesus put out his hand to help.

"Oh!" she gasped as she looked inside. And I leant over and saw something gleaming in the lamplight.

"This is gold for the king!" the man explained.

"Oh thank you," Mary said quietly as she laid the box down beside her. And Jesus reached out his hand to him.

Then another man knelt and gave her a box holding a jar wrapped in silk. He tried to explain what it was, but we couldn't understand, so he leant over and loosened the stopper. Suddenly the room was filled with fragrance.

"It's frankincense!" Mary exclaimed.

The final box also held a jar wrapped in silk, but when this was opened I recognized the smell of myrrh and remembered how Simon had given some to Mother to ease her pain.

The men were getting ready to leave while I stared at them, hardly being able to believe the gifts they'd given Jesus. They'd cost more than I'd earn in a lifetime.

I turned to the man I'd spoken to first. "Sir ... It's too much ... I ..."

He smiled. "No! This is a trifle—our tribute to the king!"

"But ... I mean .... Please tell me where you come from and how you managed to find us."

Once more, I had trouble understanding him until I managed to get him to speak more slowly. It seemed they lived somewhere east beyond the desert. One night, they'd seen a star and realized that a special king had been born in the west.

"You know, we have studied the skies for many, many years, but this is the greatest sign we have ever seen. So we came searching for him, and at last we arrived in Jerusalem. There we spoke with your King Herod; he is a learned scholar who has been to our country and knows our language!"

"But how did you find your way here?"

"Your priests have a sacred scroll that tells where the king will be born. It was prophesied that this would occur in this very village."

"So why didn't they come with you?"

He smiled. "Who knows? Perhaps they are lazy! But Herod himself will arrive soon, so that he can worship the king too!"

I shuddered; he was the very last person I wanted to meet.

"But tell me, how did you manage to find our house?"

"It was the star! We saw it again. It came and stood over where we are now."

I couldn't quite see how it could point out one house among many, but I didn't like to ask too many questions. Maybe I'd find out tomorrow.

I followed them as they went up to the inn, smiling as I saw Tom bowing and offering them the best beds in the house. Most of our neighbors were still out on the street, and as I walked back, they gave me some very odd looks. I'd have a lot of explaining to do!

Back in the house, Mary's eyes were shining. "Wasn't that wonderful, Joe, those men coming all this way just to see our Jesus? And those gifts they gave him—I've never seen anything like it!"

I nodded. "Yes, it really was amazing, but I'm afraid I can't really take it all in yet. Let's talk about it tomorrow."

We thanked God before we settled down. I'd had a heavy day and, despite all the excitement, fell asleep straight away.

CHAPTER SEVENTEEN

Then I had a nightmare and woke screaming.
I sat up and felt Mary's arm round me.

"Joe! What is it, love? Are you all right?"

"Yes, but I think I better light the lamp."

I used the little pot of fire we carried round with us. Then I saw her staring at me. "Tell me, Joe. What's happened?"

"We've got to leave here tonight! I've just seen Gabriel again and he's told me to go."

"But why?"

"It's Jesus. He's in danger! Terrible danger! We've got to get out of here now down to Egypt, or Herod will kill him!"

She didn't hesitate. "All right, Joe. I'll get everything ready."

"Look, I think I'd better go and see Eliezer. He'll tell me what to do."

As I was going out of the door, I remembered the gifts the Magi had brought, and I grabbed the boxes to show him. The street was empty, but I had a job to see where I was going as it was just after new moon. I banged on his door, scared the noise would bring a soldier along.

I was just about to give up when I heard his voice. "Who on earth's messing around out there? Don't you know it's the middle of the night?"

"It's me—Joe!" I whispered.

"Can't it wait till tomorrow?"

"No, I must talk to you now!"

I heard him swearing as he pulled back the bolts. Then at last, the door opened.

"I thought you'd had enough fun already with your visitors without bothering me! Can't you let a body sleep?"

"But it's urgent, I tell you!"

He clutched his forehead. "Oh come in then. Only keep it short! I've got a hectic day tomorrow!"

I told him about the angel. I don't think he believed me, but he didn't argue.

"So you want to go to Egypt. Well, I suppose if you're set on it, I'll have to let you go, though there's an awful lot of work on at the moment. I've got a caravan going down that way in a week; you could join them. Though why you have to wake me up to tell me I can't imagine!"

"But I can't wait that long; we've got to go tonight!"

"You're crazy! It's not safe. And anyway, what are you going to do for money?"

I pushed the boxes toward him. "Take a look at these. It's the gifts those Magi gave us."

He whistled when he saw the gold and seemed even more impressed by the spices. "Joe. Your luck's in! This little lot will keep you in comfort for a few years!"

"Well, I thought we could take it with us and sell off a bit to pay for the journey."

He held his head in his hands. "Give me strength! Don't you know what it's like out there? If anyone guesses you've got this, they'll cut your throat before you can turn round. Now just hold it for a moment; I've got to think."

I stood there feeling a fool. He went over to a table and picked up a piece of broken pot. Then he dipped a pen in some ink and started writing.

"Take this—only be careful; it's still wet. If you're really set on it, the best thing is to go to my agent in Alexandria, name of Alphaeus. He's a cousin of mine, in the Jewish quarter."

"But how do I find him?"

"Look, I've written down his address and a note to him so he knows who you are. You'll have to find your own way, and I only pray the Almighty looks after you."

"But what about this gold and the spices?"

"I think the best thing would be for me to take care of them for you. I'll give you enough money for the trip, and we'll sort the rest out later."

"But I don't know when we're coming back."

"Don't worry about that now. I'm due down in Egypt soon. I'll either bring the gifts with me or arrange a fair price."

He bustled into the next room and returned soon with a bag, which he opened to show the money inside. "Keep this hidden if you can, and just take out one coin at a time."

"I will. Oh, and one other thing. We'll take one of our mules, but I'll leave the other one here if you could get someone to look after it."

"No problem. Now if you'll excuse me, I'll get some sleep before the next drama! Perhaps I'll start seeing angels myself, or did you arrange for the emperor to turn up with all his legions?"

Mary had got everything together in bundles, and I roped them onto the mule. With my wages, I'd been able to afford two good animals. I filled a water skin from the pitcher and stuffed some bread and cheeses on top of the pack for the journey.

Then I took the lamp and had one last look round to make sure we hadn't left anything while Mary picked up Jesus, who was still asleep.

"Are you ready, Joe?"

I nodded. But suddenly I felt sorry to leave: I'd been so happy here.

"Yes, love. But I hope we'll come back soon."

There was just enough light to find our way down the street. The town gate was shut at sunset, so we looked for the hole that the shepherds had told us about. We could just about wriggle through, but the mule with its load was too bulky.

"We'll have to unload everything before we can get him out," I groaned.

Somehow, I managed to unpack in the darkness and, to my considerable relief, coax the animal through the hole, but it all took up valuable time. And just as I was roping everything back, I heard a noise. Somewhere, men and animals were on the move; there were muffled voices and a loud creaking.

"What's that?" Mary whispered in alarm.

"It sounds like they've opened the town gate for someone."

I didn't want to worry her, but I was scared it was Herod's men arriving already! I crouched down for what seemed an age. Then in the distance, I saw torches; a large caravan was heading away from the village.

Mary clutched my arm. "I think that must be those Magi we met last evening; how odd they're leaving in the middle of the night too."

"Phew! I reckon you're right. I thought it was all up with us just then! I hope they haven't woken the whole village, or it'll be much harder for us to get clear!"

But fortunately, things had quieted down and the Magi had taken the road heading east toward the Salt Sea. That suited me fine; we were going south.

I don't frighten easily, but I wouldn't like to live through that night again. There was just the two of us with the baby, and I kept wondering what man or beast was prowling in the dark. I could just make out the hills to the east and the flat top of Herodium against the sky. The thought of Herod made me want to run for my life.

Then I saw lights ahead and heard horses coming our way. I looked frantically for somewhere to hide and luckily spotted something dark by the edge of the path. It was a huge rock, and we crouched down behind it.

We were just in time. A troop of horsemen rode by almost within touching distance. I saw their spears outlined against the sky and smelt the horses' sweat; they must have been ridden fast. I hardly breathed till they had gone, praying that neither the child nor the mule would make a noise. Then at last, when I felt it safe to speak, I turned to Mary.

"One of Herod's patrols, I suppose, and going fast. I wonder what they're doing out here at this time of night?"

"I dread to think! I just hope we don't meet anymore!"

Then all too soon, the sky began to lighten. We'd made good time, and there was Hebron ahead of us with a large building glowing in the early light.

"Oh, there's Abraham's tomb," Mary whispered. "Herod rebuilt it, didn't he?"

I winced. "Yes, he did indeed. We still haven't got away from him! We must keep going as long as possible."

"But wouldn't it be better to rest here until dark?"

I shook my head. "I'd prefer to keep going while we can."

"But what if we meet more patrols? They're bound to see us in the daylight."

"They'll also find us if we stop in town."

So we went on. The country was changing; there were no more fields, just sand and rock, and when the sun rose, it felt like an oven door opening. I can still see the endless road shimmering in the heat and, on either side, row upon row of hills heaving like the sea. And all the time I kept glancing over my shoulder in case Herod's men were behind.

Once we passed some goats. Mary pointed them out to Jesus and he smiled, but what interested him more was a caravan heading north. He waved and several men waved back. One rider stopped and made his camel kneel, and then he came across to us carrying a skin.

"It's a hot day for your youngster to be out! Would he like some water?"

We thanked him very much, and he finished by giving all three of us a drink. I was grateful since it meant we could save our supply for later. Then he reached into his bag and found some dates.

"Perhaps your youngster might fancy a few of these?"

Jesus laughed as he watched the camel stand up again, complaining as it got off its knees. Then its rider urged it into a canter to catch up with the others.

Mary was smiling. "Wasn't that kind of him?"

"Yes, but I hope he doesn't tell anyone he's seen us. They'll know just where to look and then ..."

"Stop worrying, Joe! Gabriel wouldn't have told you to go to Egypt if we were going to be caught on the way!"

We stumbled on. Jesus rode perched on the mule till he started whimpering and Mary picked him up. Then I carried him on my back for a while.

Soon we were thirsty again. Every now and again, we'd pause to take a warm mouthful from our water skin, and we even found a dirty pool near the road, so the mule could drink. Once we were lucky enough to find an overhanging rock, which gave us shade while I ate a little of our bread and cheese. I gave some to Jesus, but Mary was too tired to eat.

Then I had to urge her on again. "We'll have to keep going if we're going to reach Beersheba by sunset."'

She tried to smile. But now it was a matter of putting one foot in front of the other, on and on and on. We seemed to keep walking in the same patch of sand without getting anywhere, and the sun was beginning to dip toward the hills.

By now, I was really concerned we'd have to spend the night out in the open, but then I saw some palm trees ahead. I also noticed buildings and a wall and realized we must have reached Beersheba: there were no other towns around here.

The last few steps to the well seemed to take forever, but once we'd drunk our fill, watered the mule, and filled our water skin, things felt better.

I smiled at Mary. "At least we're here. I'm glad to be in a town for the night. But we'd better watch what we say. Most of these folks are Idumeans, the same race as Herod! Some of them are related to him more than likely!"

Mary gave a tired smile. "Don't worry, Joe. We'll be all right!"

CHAPTER EIGHTEEN

"But what are we going to do, Joe?"

The sun was just setting, and we had nowhere to stay. We were on the main square and had got a small fire going. Mary was feeding Jesus gruel and trying to keep it out of his hair.

"We've just got to push on, haven't we? It's not safe to stay here."

She shook her head. "But we can't carry on like this! It's been awful today, and we're still only on the edge of the desert. It'll be a lot worse further on."

I nodded. "Well, I'm hoping I can find a caravan willing to take us."

"Can't we wait for Eliezer?"

"No, he'll be at least a week. By that time, Herod's bound to have found us!"

She took a quick look behind her. "Well, I suppose you'd better go and see what you can find. Only please hurry; I hate being in the dark by myself."

I found the caravanserai straight off and went over to the first man I saw. He was settling his camels down for the night.

"Egypt? Can't help you there, I'm afraid. We're just on our way back. But you might try those men in the corner; I think they're heading that way."

Their leader was short and stout with a bald head. He was busy giving orders, but at last he turned to me.

"What can I do for you, sir?" he said as he wiped his hands on his tunic. "Marcus is the name."

"Are you going to Egypt?"

"That's right. We're off to Alexandria at crack of dawn tomorrow! If you're up in time, you can give us a wave!"

"Would it be possible to come with you—that's me, my wife, and child?"

"No, it's not allowed, you know. You can't tell what riff raff you might pick up in a place like this; we've got some good stuff on those camels."

"But I'm not a bandit. I'm just a carpenter."

He raised his eyebrows. "Oh yes? So where've you been working?"

"Bethlehem, for Eliezer; do you know him?"

He laughed. "Yes, of course—everyone does!"

"Well, he's given me the address of his place down in Alexandria and an introduction to his agent."

Marcus took the potsherd and studied it carefully before looking up. I fancied he was a little startled.

"Sure. This looks all right. So I suppose if he's happy with you ..."

"You'll take us then? I'll make it worth your while."

He looked me carefully up and down. "You're sure you've got that sort of money? I'd need to see it first, mind!"

"I can pay you half now and the rest when we get down there."

He shrugged. "Fifty denarii for the lot of you! Take it or leave it."

I thought of the thirty coins in my bag. "Fifty?"

"That's what I said. Now if you'll excuse me, I'll get on. I haven't time to waste."

In the end, I got him down to twenty-five but he took the mule as well. He'd got a bargain there; I'd paid good money for that animal.

"I'm sorry, love," I said when I got back. "I did my best. But that tight fisted so-and-so's got most of our cash."

"Don't worry, Joe. We've more than enough, thanks to those Magi."

"Yes, but we haven't got it on us. We'll be starving by the time we see Eliezer again!"

"We'll manage, Joe! The one thing that matters is to keep Jesus safe."

She spread some robes out to lie on, but it was cold and uncomfortable.

"Try to get some sleep," I said. "I'll keep watch."

But I dropped off nearly as soon as she did; it had been a long, hard day. Then I woke up in a panic in the dark. Someone was shaking me.

"Get up, we're just off."

For a moment, I couldn't think where I was. Then I saw Marcus's face; he was carrying a torch. We were just able to grab our things and have a mouthful of water before it was time to go.

He must have done a deal with the guards for they let us out through a side gate. It was a tight fit for the camels, and the noise woke up the dogs, which ran barking and jumping up all around us. I was afraid they'd wake everyone.

Mary and I perched on two heavily loaded camels. Now we had company, it wasn't too bad travelling at night, nice and cool with a bit of a breeze. And I enjoyed watching the sky turning pale in the east before the first colors of dawn. Everything seemed so much bigger in the desert.

But we hadn't gone far when I heard a noise.

I twisted round and could just see a party of horsemen galloping behind us. They were soldiers, and I held my breath as they came abreast, praying they would not notice Mary and the child. He was asleep, and she had covered him with her robe.

They stared at each rider but did not stop. Then someone shouted an order, and they wheeled round and hurried back the way they'd come.

The men had been very quiet, but now they started talking.

"Wonder who they were after?"

"Dunno! One of Herod's escaped slaves, perhaps."

"Bah! They'd never turn out the guard for that!"

"So what about our new friends here? Maybe they were looking for them!"

I felt my guts turn to ice, but I had to say something. "You're joking! We're just working folk; do I look the type of bloke who hobnobs with kings?"

Now the chatter died away; the men were saving themselves for the long day ahead. There's no doubt about it, it takes willpower and an iron backside to ride a camel. I seemed an awful long way from the ground, and the beast walked in such an odd way, I was sure I'd fall off.

And it was agony! After an hour or so, I was wriggling, trying to find somewhere comfortable to sit. And I had several more days of this to come!

Just before sunrise, we halted for a drink, then we were off again. This is the one time the desert looks beautiful, with rocks every shade of red and pink you could wish for. But all too soon, the sun came up and the heat took over. I thought that morning would never end, but just when I couldn't take any more, we stopped for a midday break. They'd found a spot with some shade, and we drank warm water from the skin and ate some crusts.

All too soon, we were back on the camels and I got to thinking how unlucky we were. We'd been cold shouldered in Nazareth; then we'd had to drop everything at a moment's notice just when I'd got plenty of work and a nice home in Bethlehem! It was kind of those Magi to come all that way to see Jesus and they were very generous, but after all, it was them who got Herod breathing down our neck!

I even got to wondering whether I was right about Gabriel telling me to go to Egypt. Could I have imagined it? It would be just my luck if it were a mistake, and I was bouncing around on top of a camel for nothing!

I had a mind to tell Mary all this when we stopped for the night, but she was occupied telling Jesus a story. It was about my namesake Joseph, who'd been sold into slavery by his brothers.

"Poor Joseph, he was so young, but instead of riding a nice camel down to Egypt like us, he had to walk in the heat. And he had a chain on his leg to stop him running away. It was so unfair. He'd been cheeky to his brothers, but he didn't deserve this, though God helped him forgive them. And when he got down to Egypt, he soon got a lovely job looking after a big house."

"Was it like Eliezer's, Mummy?"

"No! It was much bigger! And it was owned by a very important man called Potiphar. Isn't that a funny name?" And Jesus giggled.

And she went on to say how Potiphar's wife had told lies about him and he was put in prison. Later, after he had helped two important officials by explaining their dreams, he had the chance to do the same for Pharaoh, who gave him a job ruling Egypt and he saved the country during a famine. He even had the chance to meet up with his brothers again and sort things out.

I smiled, but it really made me think. Joseph had put up with a lot of unfair things in his life, but they were all part of

God's plan to do something wonderful. My problems didn't seem anything like as bad, and God had given me something wonderful to do too, bringing up Messiah.

After that, the days seemed to fall into a pattern, and soon it felt as if we'd been traveling south all our lives. We met the odd caravan going the other way, but often it felt as if we were the only people left on earth.

But we did get some news about our friends the Magi. One evening Marcus got chatting to the leader of a caravan coming from Edom, south of the Salt Sea.

"We ran into some strange folk the other night," the man said. "Astrologers all the way from the east! And none of your usual charlatans either; they looked like princes. They even had their own caravan!"

"Hey! I think I know who you're talking about. They'd been up to Jerusalem, hadn't they? Looking for a new king born in Israel."

"That's them all right! I had a drink with one of their drivers. He reckoned they were quite mad! They'd found some peasant brat in the back of beyond and got it into their heads that this was the king they were looking for!"

"It was nothing to do with Herod, then?"

"No! Mind you, they met him in Jerusalem, and he asked if they found their king to let him know."

"So did they?"

"No. They said they saw an angel in the middle of the night who'd told them to give Herod a wide berth. So they left before dawn and headed east away from Jerusalem. The drivers had had a dreadful job rousing their camels in the dark."

Mary was most excited when I told her. "Joe! So that's why we saw them leaving in the night. I reckon it was Gabriel that warned them."

"But why were they in such a hurry?"

"Wouldn't you be with Herod waiting just six miles away? And if they had gone back to him, Jesus wouldn't have stood a chance!"

CHAPTER NINETEEN

And so at last, we came to Egypt and, to our immense relief, knew we'd finally escaped from Herod.

There's not much to show at the border, just a dried-out wadi they call the River of Egypt.

"Surely this can't be the Nile?" I exclaimed.

Aaron, one of our drivers, grinned. "Hardly! You only find water here after a storm. You'll have to wait a couple of days before we see the real thing."

Next afternoon as we traveled on across the desert, I saw some water in the distance.

"Is that part of the Nile?" I asked him.

"Oh no, those are the Bitter Lakes. I wouldn't try drinking from them; it'd take the roof off your mouth!"

Then everything changed. Instead of dry desert heat, the air became uncomfortably sticky. Scrub land gave way to fields on either side of the road with every kind of crop you could imagine. The wheat harvest was just starting.

"Look at that grain!" I remarked to Mary when we stopped for a rest. "And what an odd way to harvest it—cutting the ears off with a sickle and leaving the stalks standing!"

"It'd be quite useful if you needed straw to make bricks like our ancestors did."

"And what a funny way to dress; those loin cloths look like short skirts!"

She giggled. "I think they'd suit you, Joe!"

Then I picked up a clod of earth, crumbling it in my hand. It was a rich red.

"Good stuff, eh?" Aaron had come up behind me. "They call it the gift of the Nile. The river floods every year and carries that stuff down with it. You can grow anything you want here once you've got the water."

"But how do they get that here?"

"You see those grooves in the ground? They're irrigation channels. The locals have a gadget that helps them scoop water out of the river into them, then it runs along here. That's a tough way to earn a living—I'd rather ride a camel!"

But there was one thing I tried not to look at. We kept passing wayside shrines smothered in idols. Their lower halves looked human enough, but the heads! Ugh! It looked as if they'd been taken from birds and animals then stuck on the bodies. It was enough to give me nightmares!

Then at last we came to Memphis and the river. The city itself was on the other bank, with a small settlement this side, but there were plenty of ferries.

Aaron nodded to me. "Keep your eyes peeled; this place is full of thieves. I reckon they could take the robe off your back and you wouldn't feel a thing!"

"But why are we crossing here? I heard the men saying we're going a long way round."

"True enough, but further north towards the sea, the river breaks up into six or eight channels. If we took the direct route, we'd spend all our time getting on and off ferries! And the rates they charge!"

Once we reached the landing stage, we paused while Marcus haggled with the boat men. From nowhere, a mass of boys swarmed round us, shouting a few words of Greek, offering us fruit and trinkets, and even their own sisters! The drivers ignored them, but I bought some onions, garlic, and a couple of melons with our last coin.

While we were waiting, we went for a short stroll. The riverbanks were lined with papyrus reeds like those that grow along the Jordan, but these were much thicker.

Mary was telling Jesus how the baby Moses was put in a little basket and hidden among these reeds. "Then who should come by but Pharaoh's daughter," she said, "and when she saw the baby, she thought he was lovely and wanted him for her own son ..."

Across the river, there appeared to be some mountains glistening white in the sun, but I'd never seen any with straight edges before.

"Those are your pyramids, right enough," Aaron remarked. "Pity we haven't got time to have a proper look at them."

"They're tombs, aren't they?"

"That's right. For the old Pharaohs, so they say, though some folk believe they were built by the gods! I think they should stick one up for me when I'm gone!"

Then I saw Marcus beckoning; he'd done his deal. I looked in horror at the ferries; surely they weren't going to take us across this huge river in a reed boat! They looked so flimsy, just bundles of stems lashed together with long prows and sterns curling high over our heads.

"But they'll never take our weight, let alone the camels!" I objected.

"You'd be surprised. They'll support anything."

Aaron was right. There was a springy feel to the boat when we first got on, but it hardly sank no matter how much it was loaded. Even the camels seemed resigned to being on board, and they knelt down with a bored look on their faces.

A team of slaves rowed us across while the overseer pounded on a drum to help them keep their rhythm and swore at them to make them pull harder. We headed upriver to start with, but as the current caught us, we were swept down again. Then, just when I thought we'd finish up in the sea, we reached slack water on the other side, and in a few moments, we'd tied up. The rowers sat slumped in their seats; I wouldn't have changed places with them for anything.

Once we got everyone together, we set off again on the last leg of our journey to Alexandria. The road lay close to the river, but it was a proper Roman highway and we made good time.

I'm not a great one for the sea, but it has a nice clean smell, and after being in the sticky heat, the cool breeze was welcome. We stopped briefly in Canopus, the last town before Alexandria; it used to be the main port before that city was founded, and it still has quite a reputation.

Aaron winked at me. "Good place for a night out, Joe; they've got all the best girls here and some pretty exciting entertainment."

I shut my eyes; that was something I could do without!

As we came into the city, there seemed to be water everywhere. On our left was Lake Mareotis with the Great Sea on our right and several canals as well. We also saw a lot of big ships; most of the grain bound for Rome goes through here.

We entered the city through a large gate and came to a halt in a square. "This is as far as we go," Marcus explained. "You're in the Jewish quarter here, so you shouldn't have any problems. Just you look after yourself and that son of yours; he's a bright little kid and no mistake!"

I was wondering how to find Eliezer's agent, but the first man I asked nodded when I showed him my potsherd. "Take that street over there and the second turning on the left, under an archway. You can't miss it."

I wished we still had our mule as Mary and I staggered along with our bundles, but we found the place very quickly. The gate was open and inside was a courtyard full of camels and men sorting out huge piles of goods. A man was running around giving orders.

"I guess that's the agent," I remarked to Mary. "He looks very busy; I hope he's got time to see us."

But just then, he hurried over to us. There was no mistaking the family resemblance; he could have been Eliezer's twin.

"What can I do for you?"

"I'm looking for Alphaeus, cousin of Eliezer of Bethlehem."

"That's me."

"Eliezer suggested I came to see you. Look, I've got this message from him."

Alphaeus took the potsherd and read it carefully. "A carpenter, eh? I seem to remember him talking about you. We can certainly find you a job if you want one."

We chatted on for a bit, then he asked, "Have you been here long?"

"No, we've just arrived. A caravan from Beersheba brought us down."

He glanced at Jesus. "Quite a trip for a youngster; have you anywhere to stay?"

"No, and I'd be most grateful if you could suggest somewhere."

"That's no problem. I can fix you up myself." He turned to a youth standing nearby. "Hey Daniel! If you've got nothing to do, show these folks up to that empty room over the end storehouse. And give them a hand with their things!"

"Thank you very much, but ... eh ... there's just one thing. You see, Eliezer's got most of my money. He said he'd sort it out when he comes down, but at the moment, I'm a bit short."

"Don't worry about that. I'll lend you what you need for now, and there's a lot of work you can do if you want to start earning your keep."

Eliezer himself turned up a few weeks later. I went to have a word with him, but he simply nodded and turned away.

I didn't think too much of it at the time: he must have been tired if he'd been travelling all day and had a lot to do. But when I saw him later, he walked straight past me like he didn't know me.

"Hey Eliezer! Are you all right then?"

He half turned. "I'm sorry, Joe; I can't stop now."

"But ..."

"I'll see you later."

It didn't seem like him at all. He'd always had time to talk, however busy he was. Then as I was finishing for the day, one of his men came over. I knew him well; we'd often had a drink together. But he looked worried too.

"Joe. Got a message for you from Eliezer. He'll see you pronto down in that tavern by the causeway. Mind you, don't tell nobody where you're going."

"But why can't we meet here?"

"Don't ask me! That's what he said, and he's the boss. Know how to find it?"

"I'm not sure, but I can ask somebody."

"Well, you better get down there quick. He ain't got much time to waste."

I just had time to tell Mary where I was going. It seemed strange; the inn I knew was in the Greek quarter, not a usual spot for Jews to meet.

He was there already and gave me a half-hearted hug. "So you got down here all right, Joe? Any problems?"

"No, it all went very well—I mean, thanks to your help; otherwise we'd have been stuck. The money and the note for Alphaeus made all the difference."

"Good; only too glad to help."

He called for wine, then he sat staring at his cup. I'd never seen him so quiet; normally he'd be talking non-stop about his latest business deal.

"What's wrong?" I asked at last.

He sighed and pushed his cup away before looking up. "Plenty, I'm afraid."

He sat for a moment stroking his forehead; then, taking a quick look behind him to make sure no one was listening, he started speaking in a whisper.

"Joe, you've landed us in one almighty mess with Herod."

CHAPTER TWENTY

"Herod? But I don't understand."

"It was you and your precious Magi that set him on us."

"But we didn't do anything. We left Bethlehem that same night because an angel told me Herod was going to kill our son."

"He was right enough about that! But you don't know the half of it."

Suddenly, I felt as if a hand had clutched my throat. "So did Herod come? I think we saw some of his men."

He took his time answering, stroking his forehead again. "The day after you left, he sent in his troops. The first we knew, they were going round the houses rounding up all the children. They said they were looking for the new king."

"You mean ..."

"That's right; they were hunting for your Jesus. They took all the babies and toddlers out onto the street and started pulling their clothes up to see which were boys. And then ... and then they ..."

He started sobbing uncontrollably. Some men at a nearby table gave us strange looks, but he was too upset to care. At least we were speaking in Aramaic, and hopefully they wouldn't understand.

"I'm sorry," he said at last, "it's just that ... well, they ... they killed them."

He put his hand over mine. "Joe, it was awful. Every night I dream about it. I've seen a few things in my time, but this ... in our own village ..."

I felt myself sweating, but I had to know more. "And what happened?"

"They took the boys from their mothers and killed them right there. They even threw two or three up in the air to see who could spear them first. One woman wouldn't let her baby go, so they beat her head to a pulp! My own grandson Jason died in my arms ..."

There was a long pause while he tried to get control of himself. "I've been around a long time ... but this ..." Then he stared at me. "The awful thing is I can still hear their laughter. Those men were laughing as they did it. It was just a game for them to see who could kill the most ..."

"I'm so sorry ..." I began, but my words sounded lame.

"And it was not just us; they did the same in every village from Jerusalem down to Beersheba ... just to make sure they'd killed your precious son!"

"But why didn't you say that we'd left Bethlehem already?"

"We tried; the women kept telling them that, but it didn't make any difference. They had their orders to kill, and that was all there was to it. I suppose if they'd disobeyed, Herod would have crucified them all!"

I put an arm round him, waiting until he could compose himself. "I'm so very, very sorry. What can I do?"

He shook his head. "Nothing. If you hadn't come to live with us, those kids would still be alive. They took my grandson thanks to you, and I'm lucky I've still got a business."

"Why? Did they try to destroy that too?"

"Not them, actually, but the folk in Bethlehem. You see, they blamed me for helping you, and once the soldiers had gone, a mob went down to your place to see if you were hiding there. They smashed their way in, stripped everything, and burnt it down. They even stoned that mule you'd left behind. Then they came after me."

"How did you manage to deal with them?"

"We had to stay up all night to stop them burning my storehouses down. I've got good men, thank God, and once that lot saw cold steel, they backed off."

"But have things settled down now?"

"More or less, I suppose. But I'm still keeping a guard on my place day and night. That's why I've been so long; I should have been down here a week ago."

We sat in silence, then I said, "Do you really blame us for causing all this trouble?"

He nodded sadly. "I'm afraid so. And I think it best if we had nothing more to do with each other."

"But Eliezer—I never wanted to hurt you; you've been so good to us."

He looked beaten. "I know, Joe, and I really appreciate all you've done. But I can't see any other way out of this."

"But if we came back to Bethlehem, couldn't we sort things out? I mean, talk to everyone and try to make it right."

"Joe. You don't understand. You didn't see that mob. They hate your very guts. They'll tear you to pieces if they get half a chance. And that includes your precious child! They blame you for everything that happened, and they're not going to forget in a hurry."

"So we've just got to keep out of the way."

"Yes, you mustn't come anywhere near Bethlehem." He paused. "And I'm also worried about Alphaeus."

"Alphaeus, but why him?"

"He's got a lot of connections there, and if they knew he was giving you lodging and work, it wouldn't go down very well."

"People would be angry with him?"

"Fighting mad, more like! I wouldn't put it past them to come down here themselves to sort him out. And worse still, there's Herod; that man's got long arms. If he finds out that the young king he's been hunting for is down here in Alexandria, he'll send a murder squad to finish you off. And more than likely to finish the rest of us off too, just for the crime of sheltering you."

"But the angel told me we'd be safe in Egypt."

"You should be so long as you don't draw attention to yourselves, but no one's secure while that madman's alive."

"So what do you think we should do?"

"Move out from here as soon as possible. For everyone's sake, it would be better if you made yourself scarce."

"Where can we go?"

"Another town, maybe, but anyway keep away from the Jewish quarter till things cool down."

"We'll shift out tomorrow; we haven't got much stuff."

"That would be best. But before you leave, go past the office and pick up the money I owe you. I managed to get a good price on your gold and spices, but I suggest you keep the cash well hidden; I'd hate for you to get robbed. In fact, the sooner you get yourself another job the better, so that folks don't start thinking you're rich."

On any other occasion, he'd have been off to his next appointment as soon as he'd drunk his wine, but that evening, he didn't seem in a hurry. The moon was up, and we sat watching the sea.

"Best be going," he said at last. "May the Lord Almighty protect you and yours."

He walked up the street, and I never saw him again. I think he was the best friend I ever had.

When I got back, I told Mary what he'd said. She was too shocked to cry, so I just put my arm round her. Then I felt Jesus pushing his way in between us. I lifted him up, and we cuddled him. He was a comfort somehow.

I woke before dawn and reached out for Mary, but the bed was empty. There was a faint light and I could just see her standing by the window, so I went over to her.

"I'm sorry, Joe; I didn't mean to disturb you."

"No, you didn't. But can't you sleep?"

"No. I lay down for a bit, but it was hopeless. I've been here most of the night thinking about those little boys. I can see them all, and it's ... it's ... I just can't believe they've gone. You remember Jacob, Dinah's youngest?"

"Wasn't he a bit slow?"

"That's him. His father thought it was a waste of time feeding him since he'd never amount to anything. But she really loved him and carried him around everywhere. He was always dribbling, but she kept mopping him up and kissing him."

"Yes, I remember that."

"But did you ever see him smile? That was beautiful! And only last month, she came to me so proudly: he'd started calling her mummy for the first time ... Only now he's ... well, dead ... And I keep thinking of the games those boys used to play. I can see all their faces and their mothers' faces too. They were like sisters to me—I really get to know those mums when I saw them every day at the well!"

I felt anger boiling up. "But why kill those boys? What threat were they to Herod?"

"I don't know, Joe. I really don't."

"And how could God let it happen? Why allow a wicked old man to wipe out all those children?"

"Joe, please! God's not like that! He'd never make anyone do something dreadful!"

"But it's happened, hasn't it? All because of your son! If it wasn't for him, those children would be still alive—even

Jacob."

"Joe, Jesus is our baby, not just mine! And you can't blame God for what happened."

"So how about the Magi? If they hadn't come looking for a king, Herod wouldn't have found out about us."

Mary shook her head. "But I'm sure God called them."

"And so all those kids were murdered. And I can't forgive myself. If I hadn't pushed for us to come back to Bethlehem, this wouldn't have happened. The Magi would have gone home without causing any problems."

"No, Joe, I doubt it. They were determined to see Jesus after coming all that way, and they'd have kept looking until they found him."

"Even if he'd been in Nazareth?"

"Yes, I'm sure the star would have shown them the way."

I thought about it for a bit. "I think you're right. And I suppose Herod would have found out and killed all the little boys up there instead!"

She sighed. "I feel so sad I can't ever go back to Bethlehem. I long to see my friends again, put my arms round them, and say how very, very sorry I am. If only we could all have a good cry together, it might do something ... But it's no good; they hate me!"

"Mary! What's wrong with us? Everywhere we go, we cause trouble. I thought it was bad enough in Nazareth, but this is awful!"

"I was thinking the same last night. Then I remembered what Simeon said—you know, that old man we met in the

Temple. He warned us Jesus would cause the ruin of many people in Israel and they would hate him. And that, of course, includes Herod."

"He's a monster if ever there was one. The only thing he cares about is stopping anyone getting their hands on his throne."

"But Joe, it's worse than that. I think he's got an evil spirit!"

I shuddered, remembering how he looked at me when I was in Herodium.

"But Mary, that's awful. Jesus will never be safe now!"

She put her hand on my arm. "Joe, we've just got to trust God to look after him. He's in control."

We stood by the open window. The first grey light of dawn was showing. Then Mary spoke again very quietly.

"You know, there was something else Simeon said. He warned me I was going to have sorrow, like a sword through my heart. Tonight while I've been thinking about those little boys, I began to know what he meant. But despite all that, I wouldn't change my life with anyone; bearing Jesus is the most marvelous privilege any woman could have."

CHAPTER TWENTY-ONE

First of all, I needed to speak to Alphaeus, but I didn't want to do it in front of the men. The less anyone saw of us together, the better.

I stood in a doorway until he was free, then went and greeted him. He looked decidedly embarrassed.

"Joe, I'll come up and see you once I'm finished here."

It was a nervous wait until he appeared. I was shocked by his appearance: his face was gaunt and he seemed to have aged overnight.

"Well, Joe, I guess you know about that awful thing that happened in Bethlehem."

"Yes, Eliezer told me."

He shook his head. "I lost three nephews in that business. I still can't believe it happened."

"I know it was ... dreadful. I just don't know what to say. Herod must have been after our son, so I suppose you could say it was all our fault."

"Well ... I don't know ... I suppose we can't really blame you for what happened; it was all the work of that crazed idiot Herod. No one could have guessed he'd do something so terrible. But Eliezer thinks it would be better for the time being if you didn't live here or work for me, and I ... well, I agree with him."

"I quite understand; the last thing we want to do is to put you in danger."

"I'm really sorry about this, Joe; you're one of my best men, but you know how it is."

"Don't worry, you've been more than kind enough to us as it is. We'll leave today."

"But are you going to be all right? You're a stranger here; where are you going to live?"

"I don't know yet, but we'll find something. Eliezer reckoned we should move out of the Jewish quarter."

"Yes, I think that's wise, just in case anyone comes looking for you." Then he paused for a moment. "Look, I don't know if you'd be interested in this, but there's a Greek I do business with, name of Jason. He's more honest than most, and he's got some property down by the harbor. I'm sure he'd help if you mention my name."

"That sounds good to me. Do you think he's got somewhere we could rent?"

"Well, if he doesn't, he's sure to know someone who does. Hold on a moment and I'll write down his address for you."

He hurried out of the door, then returned with the usual potsherd inscribed in Greek. There was no time to lose, so leaving Mary and Jesus behind, I went to check things out.

Jason proved to be a very large middle-aged man who clearly enjoyed his food. He glanced at the potsherd.

"So you're a friend of Alphaeus, are you? What can I do for you?"

"Well, he's put us up—that's me, my wife, and child—in one of his storerooms since we arrived here a month or so ago. But I'd like to find somewhere more convenient, and he said you might have something I could rent."

He stood thinking for a moment. "Yes, there's one room I could offer. A family of six was living in it, but they moved out last week. It could do with a tidy up and clean, but you're welcome to it if you want."

"I'd like to have a look."

He was certainly right about the state of the place, but at least it looked dry, so we struck hands on it and I paid the first two weeks' rent. But just as I was leaving to collect Mary, he gave me an odd look.

"You must be a Jew. It seems a bit odd that you would want to live in a Greek neighborhood."

Suddenly I tensed up. "Well, I don't mind where we are. I mean, I've stayed with Greeks before."

He shrugged. "Well, as long as you pay your rent regularly and don't steal anything, it's all right by me. We don't ask many questions round here."

We moved in that afternoon. Mary didn't say much when she saw the place, but I knew she was disappointed. Eliezer had loaned us a mule to carry our stuff, and it proved useful in removing the mountain of junk left by the previous tenants. But at least once we had cleared up, there was plenty of space and even a brick stove in the corner.

I knelt down by it and started picking away at the mortar.

"What are you up to, Joe?"

"I want to loosen a brick. We need somewhere to hide that money Eliezer gave us."

We were pretty tired by the time we'd eaten, so we went to sleep early. But I woke in the dark and could just make out Mary outlined against the window.

"What's up, love? Are you still upset?"

"Yes, I'm afraid so. It's no good. I just can't get those little boys and their mothers out of my mind."

She came back to bed, but most nights after that, if I woke, I'd find her standing there. I did all I could to comfort her, but she seemed to be living in a different world. And she was hardly eating anything.

I was at my wits end. We were strangers in a foreign city, and there was nobody to turn to. But in the end, it was Jesus who made the difference. There was little time to grieve when looking after him.

He was a lively lad, much brighter than any other child I've known. He was very excited about all the new things around him, and Mary had to take him everywhere. Then when they got back, he was bursting to tell me what they'd seen. I was amazed by how many words he knew.

Next to where we were staying, there was a weaver's house, producing beautiful white linen cloth. Jesus loved to watch the women with their spindles making yarn and the men at the looms. Sometimes as a special treat, they even let him throw the shuttle.

One day he came back very excited. "Look what I've got, Daddy!" And he proudly showed a scrap of cloth they'd given him. After that, he took it everywhere except when Mary got hold of it to wash it.

Once, they went to the great library. Somehow or other, she managed to talk them into letting her inside with Jesus.

"Daddy, we saw all the scrolls! A man let me touch one!"

Mary had enjoyed it too. "Joe! You've never seen anything like it! There's room after room, piled right up to the ceiling. Oh, I'd love to read Greek! I don't think it would take me long to learn, and there's so much stuff there!"

But the harbor was his favorite spot. It was especially busy after the wheat harvest with great ships loading up grain for Rome. From dawn to dusk, a row of sweating men carried heavy baskets, which they emptied into the holds. And there was great excitement when the ships rowed out to sea and set their huge square sails.

Sometimes Mary took Jesus along the causeway to the Pharos, the famous lighthouse. It's known as one of the wonders of the world.

"Daddy, we saw a big tower. It's got a fire on top. Mummy says it tells the sailors where they are."

Once as a special treat, we all went there at night and Jesus was really excited with the huge flames lighting the sky.

Another day, I took them to the shipyards where the grain carriers are built. We watched a gang of men heaving great timbers into place to build a hull.

"I reckon there might be some work for me down here," I remarked. "They must need carpenters. Not that I know much about ships."

Mary smiled. "I'd reckon you could learn very quickly!"

I started work next day. It was different from building houses, but I picked up the methods fast enough. Before a month was out, I was in charge of my own gang.

It would be the next spring that I ran into Alphaeus down by the harbor one evening. To my surprise, he seemed glad to see me, so we went for a drink. Over some good Egyptian beer, we chatted about Eliezer and what was happening to the business. Then he gave me an odd look.

"Sounds like your old friend Herod's causing problems!"

His very name gave me the shudders, but I tried not to show it. "So what's he up to then?"

"You heard about that gilded eagle in the Temple?"

"I remember seeing one, stuck up on the wall near the Beautiful Gate. The priests were hopping mad; they reckoned it was a filthy pagan idol."

"That's the one, but it's gone now; two rabbis got their followers to hack it down."

"I bet our friend wasn't too pleased."

"You're right. By all accounts, he was in a pretty bad way, but he got up from his bed, breathing fire and brimstone, and told them to burn the ringleaders and slaughter the rest! And now there's the business of the chiefs."

"What's that then?"

"He'd invited the prominent men from all over his kingdom down to Jericho. They thought they were on to a good thing and he'd load them with gifts, but instead he's locked them all up and says they'll all get killed when he dies. I don't give much for their chances since he's very sick already!"

"That's quite dreadful—it sounds just like him. But anyway, who do you think is going to succeed him?"

"A good question—he's killed three of his potential heirs already. I hear the money's on Archelaus, though I fear he may be worse than his dad."

I left Alphaeus still staring gloomily at his drink. I felt depressed too, but that night Gabriel appeared to me again. He told me that the people who wanted to kill Jesus were dead and it was time to go back to Israel.

CHAPTER TWENTY-TWO

I shouldn't say it, but there've been times when I wondered if Gabriel got it wrong! If I'd known what we were letting ourselves in for, I'd have thought twice about leaving Egypt!

When he'd disappeared, I got up and lit the lamp. Mary stirred and opened her eyes. Then she sat bolt upright.

"Joe! You've seen Gabriel again!"

"Yes. But how did you know?"

"I could tell straight away by that look in your eyes. What did he say?"

"He told me to take you and Jesus back home. It seems all the folk who wanted to kill him are dead."

"That means Herod?"

"I suppose so, and good riddance to him!"

She looked solemn. "I know he was an evil man, but he's in God's hands now being judged! I'd hate to be in his position after what he's done."

We sat watching the lamp flickering, then she said, "Yes. Let's go."

"But where are we going to live?"

"We can sort that out later. Now Gabriel's told you it's safe to return, we might get to Jerusalem in time for

Passover."

Suddenly, something made me feel uneasy. "I don't why, but somehow I don't think that's a good idea."

"So what are we going to do?"

"I fancy taking the coast road up to Caesarea. Once we get there, we'll find somewhere to stay while we make plans."

"But Joe, you have a duty to go to the Temple for the feast if you can, and I'd like to go too."

"I know, but somehow I don't feel we should go this time."

She looked disappointed, but she didn't try to make me change my mind.

To my relief, all the arrangements for our departure went smoothly. I was worried what the overseer at the shipyard would say, but he nodded.

"So you're off then, Joe? Sorry to lose you, but any time you're down this way, look in. We've always got work!"

Then I checked the caravans heading north. There were a lot to choose from, and I took my time till I got a good price.

I came home around noon. "All fixed, Mary! We're off tomorrow, early!"

That evening, I settled up with Jason, then we packed. We still had a lot of money, so we split it between us, strapping it round our waists where it would stay hidden day and night.

The moon was still up when we left in the early hours to join the caravan. It felt odd walking along empty streets, and strangely enough, I felt sorry I wouldn't be seeing them again.

"I hope we're doing the right thing," I murmured.

"That's what Gabriel told you, didn't he?"

"Well, I suppose so. But I'd feel better if I really knew Herod was dead."

Mary pulled up short. "Now look, Joe! Did you see an angel or didn't you?"

"Well, yes ... Of course, I did."

"So then, we're doing the right thing! Come on or we'll be late."

All too soon, the caravan started off and I rediscovered the joys of camel riding! At least this time, there was plenty to see to stop me thinking about my backside. After crossing the Nile at Memphis, we headed up the ancient Way of the Sea along the coast through the old Philistine cities of Gaza and Ashkelon up toward Joppa and Caesarea.

Jesus really enjoyed the journey, and he couldn't take his eyes off the sea. "Did you build that ship, Daddy?" he asked every time he saw a sail. Then Mary told him stories of how Saul and David had fought the Philistines.

When we reached Joppa, where we were due to stop for the night, the streets were full of men milling around excitedly.

"Herod's dead!" a man called.

"Hey!" our leader shouted. "So the old bastard's gone at last!"

"May the Almighty judge him!" his informant exclaimed.

"I can hardly believe it. I reckoned he'd live forever, wallowing in that medicinal mud bath of his!"

The man was still talking as we dismounted. "... but the cream of it was his sister Salome. You know Herod had invited a lot of Jewish leaders down to Jericho?"

"Yes! But didn't he lock them up once they'd arrived?"

"That's right. He'd planned to have them killed after he'd died, to give everyone a chance to mourn! Only Salome spoilt it all by smuggling them out before anyone knew he was dead."

"Always one for his little jokes, our Herod! So who's going to be king now?"

"Archelaus, they say."

"So it is him then. Wonder how good he'll be?"

"It's hard to tell, really. From what I've heard, he wants to make a new start and keep everyone happy."

"Some hopes! The priests will twist him round their little fingers."

"Maybe, but at least he's trying. They say he's given his father the funeral to end all funerals!"

We got to Caesarea the next afternoon. It was Mary's first time there, and I thought she'd find it dull after Alexandria. But she was very excited.

"Joe! It's beautiful! Look at all that white marble!"

"We've got Herod to thank for that!"

She shuddered. "I don't know how that wicked man could build something so beautiful!"

"I don't know either. But give him his due. Before he came along, there weren't any harbors on this coast, just beach and the odd village."

We were passing the end of a great breakwater. "But Joe, he couldn't have built all this! It's huge! It must be all of two hundred paces wide."

"But he did, right enough. I remember coming down here when they were working on it. There was a whole fleet of boats lowering huge stone blocks into the sea for the foundations. The water was forty paces deep in places!"

The city was impressive too, with wide streets and a large market square near the Forum. That's where we said goodbye to the caravan, and as it was still quite early, we had a look at the stalls. I reckon you could buy just about anything there.

Most folks were Greek or Roman, but there was a Jewish quarter where we found a room for the night. Most of the men had gone up to Jerusalem for Passover, and I was feeling sorry we hadn't joined them—that is, until next morning.

We were woken by a commotion outside. There was a lot of shouting, but what really caught my ear was the wailing.

"Stay here," I told Mary. "I'll see what's happened."

She caught my arm. "Be careful, Joe! I want you back safe and sound!"

There was a huge crowd outside, and more people were joining it all the time. "What's up?" I shouted, but no one listened until I stopped an old man.

"Murder!" he bellowed. "They've killed everyone in the Temple!"

"What ... Who ...?"

But he'd been swept away by the crowd. I followed, half lifted by the mass of people forcing their way down the street. The wailing was much louder now.

We got into the Forum at last, and I could see a priest standing on a wall frantically waving to get our attention. It was a long time till the crowd quieted down, and even then, I could only hear a little of what he said.

" ... that son of Satan Archelaus ... promised us peace then slaughtered us ... thousands dead in the sacred Temple ... making their Passover sacrifice ... sent in his troops to kill and rape ... bodies piled up everywhere ..."

I was feeling scared there'd be a riot here too; if the soldiers moved in, anything could happen. But somehow, I managed to fight my way out and get back to Mary. We huddled together in our tiny room.

She was very shocked when I told her what I'd heard. "I'm sorry, Joe! You were right to come this way. Just think what could have happened if we'd gone up to Jerusalem. We'd have been stuck in the middle of it!"

"Well, I've been wondering what happened to our friends Simeon and Anna."

"I'm sure the Lord looked after them."

Near sunset, I went outside again, but now there were soldiers everywhere. "Get back indoors!" one shouted. "Don't you know there's a curfew?"

Next morning, the troops had gone. A lot of people were drifting round like sleepwalkers while others were sobbing or wailing. I passed one group of young men cursing Archelaus and swearing they were going up to Jerusalem to deal with him.

I kept asking people what had actually happened, but it took a long time before I got the full story. Archelaus had gone to the Temple to meet the people and told them he would treat them better than his father had. However, they thought he was being weak and started taking advantage. Before long, the crowd was throwing stones, and when he saw how many people were crammed into the Temple, he panicked.

He sent his soldiers in, and by the time they'd finished, there were piles of bodies everywhere, three thousand by one account, mixed up with the carcasses of the sacrificial lambs. Then the men ran riot, killing everyone they met in the streets or outside the walls. Finally, Archelaus announced that Passover had been cancelled that year and ordered everyone back home.

"Shall we go back to Egypt?" I asked Mary when I returned.

"No! We can't. You know we've been told to come here and God is going to keep us safe."

"But what do you think we should do?"

"Wait here until God shows us where to go."

"I suppose this is safer than Jerusalem. At least we don't have Archelaus breathing down our necks!"

I spoke too soon; he arrived in town next day.

There was no warning. Suddenly soldiers appeared and started lining the streets. The centurion was shouting, "Get those folk back against the wall! Move them on if you think they're planning anything and check 'em for weapons!"

"What's all this then?" somebody called from the crowd.

"Never you mind! Do what you're told or you'll get a cubit of steel in your gut!"

Then a detachment of horsemen clattered in. Close behind them were squads of foot soldiers escorting some covered litters.

"Get back there!" an officer shouted as the crowd began to surge forward, and the soldiers started beating them with the flats of their swords.

I was wedged up against a man in a rich robe. "Who's that, then?" I said when he turned my way.

"Looks like Archelaus. I guess he's off to Rome to be confirmed as our noble king!" And he spat on the ground.

"There's enough folks with him, aren't there?"

He grunted. "He must have his whole family supporting him, though I wouldn't put it past any of them to stab him in the back!"

I waited till the procession had disappeared toward the harbor and the crowd was beginning to disperse before returning to Mary.

We stayed in Caesarea one more night. I took a long time getting to sleep, listening to Mary's quiet breathing. Then Gabriel came to me one last time; he told me to take the family back to Galilee.

CHAPTER TWENTY-THREE

I never thought I'd be sorry to see the end of Herod, but at least he'd kept the peace. With him gone, the country was slipping into civil war.

Most street corners held groups of men cursing Archelaus and planning a revolt against the Romans. Whenever an army patrol passed, they'd slip out of sight only to gather again as soon as it had disappeared.

We couldn't wait to leave Caesarea, but neither were we anxious to return to Nazareth. However, there didn't seem much choice, so reluctantly, I found a caravan to take us as far as Sepphoris.

It deposited us in the forum just before sunset. It was too late to walk to Nazareth, so we settled down for the night under an archway. It was cold, and we kept being disturbed by passing patrols.

I still had my tools, so next morning I bought an old donkey to carry them; it looked just about capable of walking four miles. I'd dreaded this trip, but it was a beautiful morning and my spirits soon rose. It was fun watching Jesus darting around picking spring flowers to give us, but soon he got tired and we put him on the donkey.

When we arrived, the village looked empty since most folk were working in the fields. I greeted one old woman, but she turned her back and hobbled inside her house. And when we reached Mother's home, we found Miriam and her family had moved in.

She greeted us politely enough, but it was obvious she didn't want us living there. So I had a look at the hut I'd built when I was betrothed. It looked in a bit of a mess, but at least the roof was still on and it was dry.

Mary smiled at me. "Never mind, Joe; we'll get it tidied up in no time."

The door needed a little doing to it, and while I worked there, a lot of folk passed returning for their midday break. A few nodded, but no one stopped to have a chat or say how pleased they were to see me. Even my brother Simon looked at me as if I was a stranger.

"Well, Joe, are you stopping long?"

He was obviously still angry with me for bringing shame on the family. It left me feeling in a bad mood, but then Mary came out and gave me a searching look.

"Stop worrying, Joe! We've got to live here, so we might as well make the best of it and get on with folk if we can."

Then I thought of our neighbors. "Have you seen anything of James?"

"No, or Susannah either come to think of it."

"I suppose I'd better go round and see them."

I knocked a couple of times and got no reply, but as I turned away, James shuffled out. I hardly recognized him; he was bent over with food stains down his robe, and his eyes looked empty.

"They've gone ... Susannah ... the kids ..."

I didn't know what to say, but then his brother Elias appeared.

"What's happened?" I asked.

He looked grim. "You better come with me."

We walked down the road, leaving James standing by the door.

"It's just awful, Joe!"

He paused while he struggled to control himself. "He's lost his whole family ... Susannah ... all his children ... killed by that maniac Archelaus."

He kicked a stone viciously, and we watched it bouncing down the hillside.

"Was it that massacre in the Temple?"

"Yes. James saw the soldiers moving in, but it was too late to do anything and they didn't stand a chance. He got separated from the rest, and he was buried under a pile of bodies. That's what saved his life."

"And his family?"

"All dead! Once the soldiers had gone, he hunted through the bodies and found Susannah and all his children."

"Was he able to bury them?"

"He hadn't a hope. Archelaus ordered everybody out of the Temple, and they shoved all the bodies into one big hole."

"Oh, how dreadful!"

"Yes, he can't forgive himself for taking them down there and then not giving them a proper funeral."

However, to my great surprise, James came round to our home next day and, after that, was a regular visitor. He found Mary a real comfort.

"I don't know how you manage with him," I said one day. "I can't think of anything to say."

"I can't either. I just listen and keep an eye open. I make sure he's eating properly and has something clean to wear."

Then she looked at me. "Joe, it's odd, but this has helped me. When we were in Egypt, I kept thinking of those mothers in Bethlehem who'd lost their boys because of us. I longed to comfort them but knew I'd never get the chance."

"But now you've got James to comfort?"

"That's right." Then she turned away quickly.

"You're still upset about Bethlehem?"

"Yes," she sobbed. "I can't get those little boys out of my mind—I'm always dreaming about them! I'm reminded of something the prophet said about Rachel, Jacob's wife. He spoke of her weeping for her children and refusing to be comforted since they were dead. I wonder if that was a prophecy about what happened in Bethlehem."

Over the next few weeks, we slowly got used to life back in Nazareth. Most folk were bored with the old gossip and tolerated us, although there was little friendliness. Their real problem was they were frightened.

One day, I ran into Simon returning from a trip to Sepphoris.

"We've got to watch it, Joe! The bandits are back and have taken over the town. They even raided the armory to give weapons to the mob, and one hooligan waved a sword in my face as I was coming away. I didn't think I'd make it home!"

"Who are they anyway?"

"The usual rabble. Their leader's Judas, the son of that thug Hezekias that Herod killed thirty years back."

"But isn't this going to upset the Romans?"

"I'd say! We can expect the legions to pay them a visit any time now. And while they're at it, they'll probably finish us off as well."

"So what can we do?"

"The first thing is to hide all our food so it's not stolen. Remember that cave above the village where we used to play as boys?"

"Yes, it was quite huge, wasn't it?"

"Well, we're going to put everything in there. And if we get attacked, we can use it as a shelter; there's enough space for the whole village. But we'll have to disguise the entrance pretty well so they don't find us."

However, the next we heard was of another crisis in Jerusalem. The deputy Roman governor, Sabinus, was making himself very unpopular.

One day, Isaac stopped me. "Joe, are you coming with us to Jerusalem for Pentecost?"

"What, to offer the first fruits of the harvest?"

He snorted. "Offerings! Fat chance anyone will make any offerings this year! They've hardly had time to clear up after Archelaus's little sacrifice!"

"So why are you going?"

"To deal with Sabinus, of course! You've heard he's digging up the Temple?"

"Digging up the Temple—what on earth for?"

"He's hunting for Herod's gold! And we're going to stop him! Teach him a lesson he won't forget in a hurry!"

"What? Are you going to fight him?"

"Well, we're not giving him a party! We're throwing those Romans out once and for all. I'm taking every man in the village first thing tomorrow! Make sure you're there!"

"But hasn't there been enough killing already?"

"Bah! That's only because Archelaus caught us on the hop. This time, it'll be different. We'll be armed and we'll clear those blasphemers out pretty quick!"

"But Isaac, I can't just go and leave Mary and my child here by themselves."

He stared at me. He had funny eyes like those of the pigs the Gentiles keep. "You're scared, Joe! I always knew you were a coward. You make me sick!"

He had talked big, but he only got a dozen men to go with him, and half of those got killed, including himself. Elias was one of the lucky survivors, but even he lost an arm.

"I thought you were dead," I said. "I hear it was a disaster!"

"Near enough! You were well out of that one, Joe!"

"So what happened?"

"We had a go at the Romans all right. Thought we'd got them cornered in the Temple and outnumbered. We'd split up into three armies to surround them."

"So what went wrong?"

"They're proper soldiers, not like us! They got in formation and pushed us back, even though Sabinus, who was supposed to be in charge, was so scared he gave his orders from the top of a tower!"

"So did you make a run for it?"

"Not us brave Galileans! We're too stupid! We got up on top of the cloisters and started throwing tiles and rubbish down on them. Then the Romans got the bright idea of setting fire to the place. After that, it was every man for himself!"

"They burnt the Temple!" I gasped. I should have been upset about people dying, but all I could think of was that lovely place going up in flames.

Elias shrugged. "No, just the cloisters. I expect they'll repair them. Though I don't know where they'll find the money. Sabinus emptied the treasury while he was at it and got more than four thousand talents! We did have another go at him later, shutting him up in the palace, but then his legion cut us to bits!"

"So that's the end of it, I suppose?"

"Oh no, the place is crawling with men claiming to be Messiah and calling for a new revolt. There's bound to be fresh trouble."

We hadn't long to wait. Varus, the Roman governor, came down from Syria with two legions and four troops of horses. He took most of them on to Jerusalem, but he hadn't forgotten about Sepphoris and sent in his friend Caius to deal with it.

One morning, Simon came beating on our door. "Joe, the Romans are here! I've just seen their army—we better hide quick!"

Soon the village was empty with everybody up in the cave. The next two days were awful, sweating in the dark, and the whole place stank thanks to the animals. But worst of all was the sense of panic. Eventually, I'd had enough, and slipping out, I went up the hill taking care to keep down behind the rocks.

There was a huge pall of smoke over Sepphoris. I learned later that the Romans had burnt it and enslaved everybody they could find. Down on the other side of the hill, I could see a long line of men and women in chains trudging slowly toward Sebaste. If they were lucky, they'd be sold in the market as personal slaves; otherwise, they'd finish up rowing a galley or working down a mine.

But it was nothing to what happened in Jerusalem. Varus made short work of the rebellion by crucifying two thousand Jews. I've seen a few executions in my time, although they always make me feel sick. I can't imagine how anyone would want to inflict such pain on another person. But when I thought of two thousand men suffering together, I felt quite numb, overwhelmed by the awfulness of it.

Varus had achieved what he set out to do—restoring a sort of peace to the country—but he left everyone hating the Romans. From now on, most Jews would bide their time until they could finally defeat their oppressors.

Ten years on, this moment may be near; we've just heard that Varus is dead. He committed suicide after losing a crucial battle while trying to pacify a new province in Germania. The local tribes ambushed three legions and wiped them out completely. The Jews here are celebrating his death, but the Romans are looking rather nervous. I think they're wondering how much longer their empire's going to last.

CHAPTER TWENTY-FOUR

But I'm getting ahead of myself. One evening soon after we got back to Nazareth , Mary looked at me. "Joe. I've got something to tell you."

"What? Nothing bad, I hope!"

She giggled. "You always think the worst! No, it's lovely!"

"So what is it then?"

"I'm expecting another baby!"

"You don't mean you've ..."

She laughed louder. "No, Joe. I haven't seen Gabriel again! This one's yours!"

"Mine? Is it really?"

"Well, whose do you think it is?"

I went to grab her, but she pushed me away.

"You've got to be careful with me now, Joe!"

"I will. That's great news! I wish I could have told Mother; she'd have been so proud."

This news came as a relief to me; I'd been worried I might never be a proper father. But next summer, she presented me with my very own son. I called him James.

Once the village midwife had done her stuff, I smiled down at Mary and James lying in the new bed I'd constructed. "Well, at least this time you've got somewhere clean to have your baby!"

"Yes, I can't say I miss the cows!"

I leaned down and picked James up. "Isn't he beautiful? He'll make a proper carpenter just like his dad!"

"I'm sure he will. But why don't you go and find Jesus? He's longing to see his new brother."

He came in rather shyly and stood for a long time gazing at James. Then very gently, he reached out his hand and stroked his head.

I'd been wondering how he'd take to the new baby after being an only child for so long. But he couldn't have been better; he was always watching him and leaning over the cradle to chatter. There was no jealousy about him at all.

Then our neighbor James looked in to see his namesake.

"Another good-looking lad you've got, Joe. But where are the angels?"

"Angels? What are you talking about?"

"Well, I thought they always turned up to see Mary's babies!"

I looked him in the eye, but he just laughed. "We've heard all about your goings on in Bethlehem!" Then he put his face close to mine. "Only I hope we don't get our boys killed because of your youngster!"

"There's no danger of that now Herod's dead!" I insisted.

The birth of James did a lot to make people more friendly with us, and there was a constant stream of women eager to see him. Jesus helped a lot too; no one could resist such a cheerful, lively little lad.

One of his favorite spots was my workshop, and he'd watch me for hours. I made him some tools of his own, and he carried them around everywhere. He proved good with his hands, and soon he was making toys out of scraps of wood for the other children.

Then one day, he disappeared. We were getting very worried when Ezra came down the hill holding him by the hand.

"Here's your daddy, young man!" he said, then he turned to me. "You've got a fine rabbi there, Joe!"

"Oh I am sorry! I hope he's not been a nuisance—we didn't know where he'd got to."

"He's been no trouble. He's been listening to the boys doing their Hebrew lessons, and to my amazement, he even knows his letters!" Then he said rather more quietly, "Just like his mother before him." I think he was still embarrassed about the way he'd treated her.

"Thanks very much for bringing him back," I said. "We'll make sure he doesn't bother you again."

"Oh no! Please do not stop him coming to me. The finest thing that a child can do is to study the law."

After that, Jesus was always up at synagogue, and although he was very young, he became the star pupil. But the other boys didn't resent him as he was so enthusiastic that he made the lessons fun.

By now, we had our hands full. Mary had had another boy and we called him Joseph after me. My friend James had remarried, choosing a nice quiet girl from the next village, so there should soon be another family for our children to play with.

Mary then had a further son, but sadly he died when he was only two days old. Then came Simon, followed by two girls, and Judas last of all. I don't mind saying I was very proud of them despite all the squabbling you expect with families.

But the strange thing was that Jesus never got into any of the rows; in fact, he sorted them out. It was a mystery how he did it; maybe it was the calm, firm way that he spoke. And we soon started leaving him in charge when we went out. So it was odd that it was he of all our children who gave us the biggest fright.

He was twelve and had just read in synagogue for the first time. Many parents sweat, afraid their boy will mess it up, but Jesus took the scroll like he'd been doing it for years and didn't make a single mistake.

He was very keen to come with us to Jerusalem for Passover now that he was counted as a man. Mary hadn't been for years because of the children, but her sister Joanna offered to take the younger ones off her hands while we were gone.

We went the usual route through Sepphoris to the Sea of Galilee then down along the Jordan Valley. Jesus walked with me for a bit, but then he joined the other boys. Often, they would lag behind, then suddenly run past us and go on far ahead.

"I wish I had their energy!" I said to Mary.

I kept an eye on Jesus for the first couple of days as it's easy to get separated. But as he seemed responsible, I decided it was only necessary to check up when we stopped for the night.

One thing I really enjoy about these trips is how everyone seems happy and excited, freed from their usual chores. Even at the end of the day when we were tired, someone would start singing a psalm and we'd all join in.

We did this too, particularly as we reached the end of our journey and descended the Mount of Olives. We could see the Temple gleaming in front of us still looking as beautiful as ever. They must have done a lot of repairs since that Sabinus riot.

As ever, the city was crammed with pilgrims, but fortunately we had a place to stay. Mary had a relative, Micah, who gave us a floor to sleep on, and we'd agreed to share the Passover lamb with him and his family. He'd already picked an animal out, and we just had to collect it after it had been sacrificed.

"I'm sorry. It's a terrible price this year!" he apologized. "But it was a job to get one at all; there're more pilgrims here than ever all wanting their lamb."

When we got to the Temple, there was hardly room to breathe. But I found Jesus a spot next to a pillar with a wall to stand on so he could watch everything over the heads of the crowd.

There were so many lambs that it took a long time to sacrifice them all. The priests stood in two rows holding bowls to catch the blood, gold on one side and silver on the other. Then they passed these down the line so the blood could be thrown against the altar. In the meantime, we sang psalms and some priests blew rams' horns. I reckon they could have heard us back in Nazareth!

We got our lamb eventually and began the slow walk through the crowds, out of the court, and across the bridge. Inevitably, we kept being jostled, and Micah, who was carrying the lamb, was nearly knocked over.

We held the feast in his house. I still enjoy all the tradition and preparations, searching by lamplight for any yeast that's still in the house and clearing the floor so we can put our food down. And there's that wonderful smell of roasting lamb; we don't get to eat meat very often and we really look forward to it.

After we've drunk the first of the four separate cups of wine, we clear things away. Then the head of the household retells the story of how our ancestors left Egypt. But to do so, he needs the help of the youngest child there.

This was Jesus, so he asked him the traditional questions: "Why are we holding this feast?" and, after pointing to each special dish in turn, "Why are we eating this?"

Each item is meant to remind us of something. For instance, there is salt water for tears and bitter herbs for slavery. We follow the same ritual each year, but this time Jesus was so excited that it made it seem fresh.

We were due to return home next day, but we sat up talking till late and then inevitably overslept.

"We've got to hurry or they'll go without us!" I urged Mary.

But she smiled, "Don't worry, Joe; we'll get there all right."

Clearing up and packing seemed to take longer than usual. Then as we were leaving, Mary asked, "Have you seen Jesus anywhere?"

"He was here a moment ago; he must have gone on ahead. We'll see him when we meet the others."

We just got there in time; our fellow pilgrims were already picking up their things, ready to go.

"Has anyone seen Jesus?" Mary asked.

A woman turned round. "He'll be up there with the other lads. I saw him talking to my Daniel."

So we set off, stopping for the night a few miles north of Jericho. As Mary was getting our food together, she said, "Give Jesus a shout, I'm almost ready."

I went over to the boys, but he wasn't with them. Then I hurried round the other groups, but no one knew where he was. It's what every parent dreads—a missing child! One of the men thought he'd seen him walking on ahead some time before, but he couldn't be sure.

"You wait here, Joe," Mary said as I returned empty handed. "I'll have a look myself."

CHAPTER TWENTY-FOUR

She didn't have any luck either and was crying when she came back.

"Joe! He's lost. He must still be in Jerusalem. We've got to go back for him now!"

"But we can't. It'll be dark in a moment."

"Joe, I'll never forgive myself if anything's happened to him!"

Somehow, I managed to stop her marching off straight away, and instead we lay down, but neither of us got much sleep.

CHAPTER TWENTY-FIVE

We started back at first light. Simon was stirring, so I explained what we were doing. Then Mary added, "Could you ask Joanna if she'd be kind enough to look after our children a bit longer?"

He looked very worried. "Oh yes, of course, but I do hope you'll find him. Take care you two, and may God direct you."

Soon after we had set out, we began to meet pilgrims heading north after the feast. We asked each group about Jesus, but nobody knew anything.

Then Mary turned to me. "I'm sure he's hurt himself! He must be lying by the road."

"Oh, somebody will be sure to be looking after him," I replied, trying to sound confident. "We'll check at Jericho; that's where he's most likely to be."

We spent some time asking round there, but there was no news, so we began the long, slow climb up to Jerusalem. At that time of year, there were spring flowers and grass in among the rocks, but neither of us was in the mood to enjoy them.

Pilgrims were still coming down from Jerusalem, but mostly the road was empty. I kept an eye open for bandits, but hopefully they wouldn't think us rich enough to rob. I didn't say anything to Mary, but I could see her gazing round too.

When we reached Jerusalem, it was late and the city gates were just closing. I reckoned the most sensible thing would be to go back to Micah's home because if Jesus was still in Jerusalem, he might have found his way there.

We had to knock several times before he unbolted the door. Then he stared at us. "What are you doing here? I thought you were halfway home by now!"

"We've lost Jesus, and we're looking for him! Have you seen him around?"

Suddenly, he was very concerned. "Well no, I'm afraid I haven't. Let's think ... the last time I remember seeing him was two nights back when we had Passover. I thought he was with you."

Mary burst into tears, so he said, "You better come in; in fact, you might as well stay here tonight. It's too late to do anything this evening, but you ought to be able to find him tomorrow. He's a sensible lad, and I doubt he's gone far."

But even as he spoke, I could see the worry in his eyes.

We combed the city next day; now that most of the pilgrims had gone, it was easier to move round. Again and again, we would see a boy who looked like him, only to be disappointed when we came up close.

We walked all the streets and checked the markets. None of the stall holders or beggars had seen him, and when we asked some Roman soldiers, they just shrugged: one Jewish boy looks like another to them.

We went back to Micah's and stayed another night. We'd got nowhere, and the longer this went on, the less chance there seemed of finding him. I was sure he must have had an accident or been kidnapped.

But there was one fear I didn't share with Mary. Perhaps a Roman officer with a taste for young boys had fancied him. Once he'd had his fun, perhaps he'd kill him or turn him out on the street. No respectable person would want to know him after that; he'd never be welcome back in Nazareth.

"So what do we do now?" I asked Mary next morning.

"I suppose we could try the Temple again."

We'd already had one look. The trouble was that it was so huge and crowded, I doubted we'd ever spot him, even if he was there.

We walked slowly along the southern colonnade. It's known as Solomon's porch, and there are a series of alcoves between the pillars where the rabbis do their teaching with their disciples gathered around them.

On previous visits to the Temple, I'd paused and listened to them. Not that I understood their scholarly talk, but it was interesting all the same. However, that morning we felt desperate and moved on quickly from one group to the next.

I was all for giving up by the time we reached the corner. In the last alcove, there was a lively debate going on. Then all of a sudden, I heard a familiar voice.

"Mary, it's him!"

There he was sitting close to the rabbi, in among his disciples, looking a bit grubby, but none the worse for the last three days. He was obviously enjoying himself, discussing some tricky point from the law almost as if he were chairing the discussion himself and quoting the Torah with the best of them.

Then he looked up and saw us. He smiled and nodded before turning away and asking another question. The rabbi looked very thoughtful.

We were flabbergasted. I knew Jesus was bright, but I'd no idea he could argue like this.

Then Mary stirred. "Joe, I think you'll have to go and get him out."

I edged my way nervously through the crowd. When he saw me, he smiled and stood up. He said something to the rabbi, then followed me back to Mary.

She hugged him, crying her eyes out. Then at last, she let him go. "Jesus! How could you? Running off like that! Your father and I have been hunting for you for days! We thought something dreadful had happened!"

Any other boy would have squirmed or looked embarrassed, but he just seemed to be puzzled. "Didn't you realize I've got to be in my Father's house?"

What an odd thing to say! It didn't make sense. I was his father—well, his adopted father anyway, and my house was back in Nazareth.

However, Mary was still crying and the last thing I wanted was a scene in front of these scholars. But as we were turning away, the rabbi beckoned to me. I hung back, but he gestured again and Mary urged me on.

"Is this your son?"

"Yes, sir. I hope he's been behaving himself!"

"Indeed he has. In my whole life, I have never heard so young a boy with such understanding and knowledge. He is a credit to you."

"Well, thank you, sir."

Then another man spoke. "I would be surprised to hear many rabbis speak as well as him. He has a rare gift!"

Several of the others agreed, though I did see one or two who looked a little sour.

But as we walked away, I suddenly felt angry and wanted to beat him for running away like that.

"Wait till I get you back to Nazareth, young man!" I warned.

Mary said nothing; she was trying not to cry. But when we reached Micah's house, she broke down again, hugging her son and sobbing and sobbing.

At last, she pulled herself together. "I'll get you something to eat."

"Thanks, Mum."

"He doesn't deserve it!" I growled.

"Oh Joe! Look at him! The poor lad's starving!"

She got him some bread and fish, and he really tucked in. I don't know what he'd eaten the last few days, but it couldn't have been much.

I sat and glowered. "Now thanks to you we've got to find another way to get back to Nazareth! I don't fancy walking all that way by ourselves!"

"We'll find somebody," Mary said, and she was right. Micah heard of a group going back to Capernaum next day. They'd been delayed in Jerusalem because their leader was sick.

So once again, we started off for Jericho. I was still angry and not in the mood to talk, so I was relieved when he went and joined some of the other lads at the front of the group.

We trudged on in silence. I could feel Mary bursting to say something, but I ignored her. Then she took my arm. "Don't be too hard on him, Joe."

"Why? I've got every reason! Look how he's messed us around!"

"It's our fault more than his. We should have checked he was with us when we left!"

"But he's old enough to behave!"

"Joe, love, he's only twelve! Didn't you do silly things at that age?"

I grunted. "Not like that!"

"I wonder! But aren't you glad to get him back safe and sound?"

"Of course I am. You know how worried I was—but what about all our other kids?"

"They'll be all right with Joanna for a bit longer."

"And what about me? I've just lost three days' work! We can't afford to throw money away like that! And folk will start taking their jobs elsewhere if I'm not around!"

"Everyone knows you do a good job. They'll wait for you."

"But it was so stupid of him! If only he'd told us what he was doing instead of wandering off like that!"

"Joe, please listen to me. I've been talking to him! He didn't mean to upset us."

"Not upset us! Lads are all like that nowadays! No respect for their elders!"

"Oh, that's not true, Joe! He's only too anxious to help; he never argues with you or disobeys. And he's upset about the anxiety he's caused."

"But why did he do it for goodness sake?"

"God's so real to him that he wanted to spend more time worshipping him in the Temple and he forgot everything else."

"What do you mean real? Isn't God real to us too? Why do you think we've been to Jerusalem if it wasn't to worship?"

"Yes, but there's something different about him. He's talking to God all the time as if they're standing next to each other."

"I thought all children did that. They've got their make-believe friends no one else can see."

"No, it's not like that at all. I know he's really hearing from God."

"Well, aren't we? I mean, we've both seen Gabriel!"

"Yes. But that was just on special occasions. It's happening to him all the time. Watch him and you'll see what I mean."

"He looks normal enough to me!"

"Well, there's something different about him. He may be our son, but it's almost as if he's ... well, in charge of everything!"

We walked on in silence. I could see Jesus at the front of the group and was very glad he was safe. Maybe I had been a bit hard on him.

I got to thinking. What with working all hours to make ends meet, I'd taken him for granted recently, just someone who would join the family firm. I'd almost forgotten the amazing things that happened when he was born.

Now he was growing up and getting his own ideas. But far more than that, suddenly I realized that God was preparing him for something really special, and I better go along with it.

That evening when we stopped, I went and put my arm round him. "Good to have you with us, son."

He didn't say anything, but somehow, I felt things were all right again.

CHAPTER TWENTY-SIX

I was coming to rely on Jesus more and more in the workshop. Mind you, he hadn't reached his full strength yet, and when there was something really heavy to shift, I had to ask someone else. But most jobs he did as well as me.

After a year or so, I'd forgotten that spot of bother in Jerusalem, till one day I happened to overhear his brother James chatting to him.

"Hey Jesus, so you were out again last night?"

I didn't take much notice then as I was busy, but later I started wondering. So I decided to have a word with James.

"What was that you were saying to Jesus this morning? You know, about being out at night?"

He shrugged. "Oh nothing."

"But I heard you ask him why he had gone out."

"Well, Dad, I didn't want to say. But last night, he wasn't there. You know, in bed."

"Are you sure about that?"

"Course! The moon was up, and I could see as plain as anything he wasn't there."

"He'd probably gone out to relieve himself."

"Can't have. The straw was cold; he must have been gone for hours!"

"Did you see when he got back?"

"No. I was asleep. But he was there when I woke up. I reckon he'd been out to see that Rachel."

"Rachel? What, that girl who lives down the street?"

"Yes, her! Got her eye on him she has. Keeps hanging around every time we come out of synagogue."

"So what's he think about her?"

"Dunno. He never tells me anything!"

I suppose I should have asked Jesus himself, but it was all a bit personal. However, a few days later, young James sidled up to me, looking disappointed.

"It wasn't her, Dad."

"What?" I hadn't the faintest idea what he was talking about.

"It wasn't Rachel, Dad."

"Rachel? What are you on about?"

"You know, why Jesus goes out at night. He wasn't going out to see her."

I put down my plane and stared. "I think you better explain yourself!"

"Well, Dad, I woke up last night and I could see him creeping around. Then he climbed down the ladder and went out. So I followed him."

"You mean you went outside?"

"Yes, Dad. Up the hill."

"Look, James, I don't want you wandering round the village in the middle of the night. It's not safe!"

"Don't worry, Dad. I've done it hundreds of times."

I let that go. "So what was Jesus up to then?"

"That's the funny thing. He just went up to that rock beyond the synagogue and lay down beside it. Praying he was."

"Praying?"

"Yes. He was stretched out flat. I got on the other side of the rock, and I could hear him at it. On and on, talking to his Father, it sounded like. I suppose he must have meant God, but it's a funny way to pray! But what got me about it was he was so excited; it was like the two of them were there together having a really good talk."

"How long was he there?"

"Dunno. I waited for a bit. But I got bored, and I was pretty cold. So I cut off back home."

I kept an eye on Jesus that day. I reckoned if he'd stayed out most of the night, he wouldn't be up to doing his work, but he seemed just the same as usual. He even tidied the workshop for me when we'd done because he said I looked tired.

I told Mary about it that evening and it set her thinking.

"So perhaps he does need a girl to settle him down. That Rachel might just be the right one."

"But he's far too young to start thinking of that!"

"I don't know so much; you were his age when you started making eyes at me!"

It was true; I hadn't realized how quickly the years had gone. Then she smiled at me. "Don't worry, Joe. I'll have a word with him."

It was a couple of days later when she came round to the workshop looking thoughtful.

"Joe, I asked Jesus about Rachel."

"Oh yes. So what did he say?"

She shook her head. "There's nothing doing there. He was very surprised when I mentioned her. I don't think the thought of marriage had crossed his mind."

"But she seems a nice enough girl. He could do worse."

"Maybe. But he's just not interested. In fact, he's not thinking of getting married at all at the moment."

It was my turn to be thoughtful. "You don't think that he's ... well ..."

"Oh no, it's nothing like that. It's just that he's got other things on his mind."

"You mean like being Messiah?"

"That's right. And I think what he really wants is to pray and study the Scriptures with Ezra anytime he's free."

"I only hope he's not going to finish up like one of those Pharisees, work all day and study all night till their wits get addled."

"I don't think you need worry about that, Joe! He's got his feet firmly on the ground. But I do wish sometimes there were some way of making him take life a bit easier."

Then one afternoon, I was just standing outside the house when James came by with a black eye.

"What have you been up to?" I said.

He mumbled something and went inside Then young Joe came along too.

"What's up with James, then?" I asked.

"Oh, nothing much. He's got in a fight. Some of the kids picked on him."

"But why did they do that?"

"Oh, they keep laughing about us because of Jesus. I'm sick of it! They're always asking us how Messiah is today, or then they tell some dirty jokes about ..."

His voice trailed off, but I knew what he meant. No one had forgotten the scandal of his birth.

Suddenly he looked up at me, clenching his fists. "I hate him! Why can't we have a normal brother like everyone else?"

***

Well, that's it really; I'd have liked to say more, but I'm afraid my time's up.

I've been lucky all these years, strong as an ox, never had a day's illness. But last autumn after the Feast of Tabernacles, I got a fever. I couldn't shake it off for weeks, and all winter I've been good for nothing. I don't reckon I'll see another summer.

I can just about walk as far as the workbench. And here I sit thinking about Jesus and wondering what he's going to do. He's in charge of the workshop now and doing a good job. Mind you, I don't know how he manages. I've never known anyone get by with less sleep; I only hope he doesn't try to do too much.

I must admit I can't imagine him being a carpenter forever. I reckon he'll make his mark somehow, though I don't know what sort of Messiah he'll be. But, somehow, I can't see him getting an army together to throw the Romans out.

And there's Mary. I've got this feeling in my bones that things are going to be very hard for her. These last few weeks, I keep remembering what Simeon said all those years ago, about a sword piercing her heart. I only wish I could be around to help her when it does, but I'm afraid she'll have to carry that alone.

Yet, you know, she's the same old Mary. She may have gone grey, but she's still so alive, just like that first time I noticed her. Somehow, I'm sure she's going to come through it all.

I'd give anything in the world to see what'll happen. I reckon it'll be exciting.

Made in the USA
Columbia, SC
21 November 2022

71164379R00126